With Love From Wolf Falls

Second Chance Fates
Book 1

Ginny Danes

Copyright © 2025 by Ginny Danes

All rights reserved.

No part of this book may be reproduced in any form or by any electronic or mechanical means, including information storage and retrieval systems, without written permission from the author, except for the use of brief quotations in a book review.

Cover Designed by Carly Beyer

Developmental, Copy, and Line Editing by @claritycopyco

Proofreading and Formatting by @kmortonedits

e-Book ISBN: 979-8-9945531-0-7

Paperback ISBN: 979-8-9945531-1-4

To the ones who found the right thing at the wrong time.

Chapter One

Natalie

It was one of those days—the kind that starts way too early and makes you want to curl into bed before the sun is all the way up.

"Mommy! Mommy! Get up! It's camping day!" a little voice shouted before a heavy weight landed on top of Natalie. She groaned as she opened her eyes and checked the clock: five a.m.

"I know you're excited, Emma, but we don't need to be up quite so early," Natalie explained to her daughter.

"But Mommy, it's camping day. We need to go *camping*," Emma argued. Natalie had to admit, the little girl was convincing. It didn't take much once she turned on the charm.

"Yes, Emma, it's camping day," Natalie conceded. "Come on, let's go then."

After breakfast, Natalie finished up the last-minute packing. She hoped she wasn't forgetting anything, even though it seemed like she'd packed all but the kitchen sink.

Fitting everything in the minivan felt like doing a very complicated jigsaw puzzle.

"Noah, did you pack enough books to read? It's a long drive," Natalie asked her son as she poured a cup of coffee.

"Yeah Mom, and I can always reread them," Noah responded, setting his backpack by the door.

When Natalie lowered her mug, she saw a giant unicorn bouncing down the hall. "No, Emma, you can't bring Sprinkles. She's too big."

"But *Mom*, she's my *favorite*."

"She's too big, honey. You'll have to pick a smaller lovey to take."

A disappointed unicorn bounced back down the hall. Emma returned with three smaller stuffed animals, which Natalie allowed. With the kids loaded and the van stuffed to the brim, it was time to hit the road and leave the city behind. Their destination: a small campground deep in the woods.

With forty-three sites nestled in the mountains of West Virginia, the campground was surrounded by trees on three sides. On the fourth side was a beautiful wide river with water so clear you could see all the colored rocks that peppered the bottom. The sites were private, with thick trees and brush in between each one, to the point where you almost felt like you were camping alone. The only things keeping the campground from being classified as "rustic" were the electricity running to each site and the indoor plumbing.

The drive was five hours in the car, with the kids fighting and whining most of the way.

"Are we there yet?"

"How much longer?"

"I'm *hungry*."

"I have to go potty."

Once they finally arrived at the campground, it took a couple more hours to set up camp in the summer heat. The kids released their pent-up energy chasing a ball around while Natalie attempted to assemble the four-person tent. She was worried her two wild things would disturb the quiet afternoon, but the trees blocked most of the sound.

"Emma, don't kick it so hard," Noah scolded as his sister booted the ball at her brother.

"I didn't!" Emma defended as she then kicked the ball out into the road.

"*Emma!*"

"I didn't mean to! I'm just too strong."

Natalie stopped sorting tent poles to intervene. "Emma, honey, please try to kick more softly. Noah, trade places with her so she's not kicking into the road. I need to get this tent up before dark."

As she struggled with the tent, Natalie decided she really should have practiced setting it up before she left. She had looked over the instructions and thought it looked easy enough, but putting it into practice was another story.

Once the tent was up and she was relatively sure it wasn't going to fall on them in the night, she began unpacking the rest of the van. *Why do three people need so much stuff?* Natalie didn't have time to think of an answer while she set up sleeping pads and bags, then opened chairs around the firepit. The kids had moved on from their ball game to searching for bugs and other critters.

By early evening, the kids had settled down and Natalie was exhausted. The coffee she'd had early that morning had worn off long ago. When the kids started grumbling about being hungry, Natalie covered the picnic table with the cheap plastic tablecloth she brought and began preparing dinner. She brought out the covered bowl of tuna salad and some paper plates, but when she went to grab the chips, they were nowhere to be found.

"Hey, kids," she called out. "Did one of you take the bag of chips?"

"No," both kids replied at the same time.

After searching all the totes and bags, Natalie gave up and went to the cooler for drinks—but she found the chips instead. She set them on the table and opened Emma's juice box, but before she could sit down, the juice was running all over the table and she was running for the paper towels.

"I'm sorry, Mommy," Emma cried.

"It's okay, honey, it was an accident," Natalie comforted as she cleaned up the juice. A little spilled juice wasn't worth her daughter's tears. They'd had enough of those lately.

Natalie had finally sat down and was scooping salad onto her plate when a gust of wind blew through. She scrambled to hold down as much as she could on the table when Noah spoke.

"Mom? Isn't that part of the tent blowing toward the river?"

Sure enough, the rain guard from the tent had detached and was on its way to test its waterproofness in the river. The kids laughed as Natalie chased the cover one way and then another while the wind blew it around. But Natalie wasn't laughing. In fact, she was close to tears.

By the time dinner was cleaned up and the campsite was secure, it was already past bedtime. Natalie wiped the dirty hands and faces of her children, tucked them into bed, and read them a story. It wasn't long before they were both sound asleep.

With the kids asleep in the reassembled tent and a

struggling fire going, Natalie curled in her chair to reflect on the day, tears streaming down her face. This wasn't how it was supposed to be.

"We need to talk, Lee," Dave had stated two months ago after walking in the door without so much as a hello.

Natalie hated that nickname. She had an uncle named Lee, so it always sounded masculine to her. There weren't any other pet names between them—it was always just Lee.

"Sure, Dave. Let me just finish up these dishes and I'll meet you in the living room." She and the kids had already eaten dinner and she was cleaning up while the kids played quietly in their rooms. She heard Dave pour himself a drink while she finished loading the dishwasher and wiped down the counters. After picking up a few toys on her way to the living room, Natalie finally settled into the couch. Her heart pounded as she wondered what Dave could want to talk about. He didn't keep her waiting, cutting right to the chase.

"Lee, I think we need some space. This situation isn't working for me anymore. I've rented an apartment close to the office. I'll be staying there for a while."

Natalie's heart broke in an instant. *Situation? Is that what this is now?* She thought Dave would want to talk about something that needed to be done around the apartment, or maybe something that was happening at work. She never expected this.

Without giving her a chance to respond, he headed into the bedroom and came out with two packed bags. He grabbed his jacket and briefcase, handed her a paper with an address on it, and said, "This is where I'll be. I'll call tomorrow to work out a schedule for the kids." With that, he walked out the door with Natalie's jaw still on the floor.

At first, Natalie tried to talk to Dave, to work things out, but he wouldn't even return her calls. She didn't understand what had brought them to this point. Dave had lost his job due to downsizing a month after she had booked the camping trip. He'd searched for months before finding his current position. She knew he was stressed at the new job, but to give up on ten years of marriage so easily—she couldn't believe it. He hadn't even given a reason before walking out.

As their vacation grew near, she needed to make a decision. After another failed attempt to get a hold of Dave, she decided to take the kids camping on her own. Noah was taking the separation especially hard. He'd retreated into a shell, and Emma just kept asking when Daddy was coming home. Natalie had explained that their dad needed some time while he adjusted to his new job, but that didn't help them understand why they couldn't see him at all. The truth was, he hadn't even tried.

They could all benefit from getting away.

So here they were, on what was supposed to be their family vacation—a vacation she'd planned six months ago with her husband and kids. A week of camping, fishing, hiking, swimming, and enjoying the outdoors sounded like a great way to close out the summer and reconnect as a family. Now, Natalie wondered if this was how life would be from now on. Would it always be just the three of them? How would she support them when Dave had been the breadwinner? Would it always be this hard?

Her thoughts drifted as she gazed into what had become a poor excuse of a campfire, thinking of what was and dreaming of what could have been. She was too physically and emotionally drained to bother building a better fire, but at the same time, too wired to sleep. She was so lost in her thoughts that she was startled when a large figure suddenly appeared in the light in front of her.

"Excuse me, miss," a man's voice said. "It looks like you're having some trouble with your fire there. Mind if I take a look?"

Natalie just stared. Even in the dark, she could tell the man was attractive. As he moved closer, she let her gaze travel up his muscular six-foot frame and into his piercing green eyes that almost looked like they glowed in the firelight. He was the type of man that she felt had no business talking to her.

"I'm Officer Lake, the ranger on duty down at the station," he continued as he ran his fingers through his dark hair. When Natalie didn't respond, he began picking up some sticks and dry leaves from the treeline. He used a long branch to arrange her logs and the kindling he'd added. Soon, he'd built an actual glowing fire that eased the chill that had grown in the air. However, for Natalie, it wasn't just the fire providing the heat.

Jackson

A loaded-down minivan pulled away from the ranger station as Jackson returned from bathroom duty. Cleaning the bathrooms had to be his least favorite part of being a park ranger, though it wasn't the worst thing he'd ever had to do. He'd spent the last few years cleaning up after sick animals. He'd gotten burnt out on the chihuahua check-ups and poodle pedicures he was assigned as the assistant vet for an animal hospital in the city. When the practice went under due to the owner's corrupt business dealings, Jackson Lake took the opportunity to step away from the city for a while and applied to be a summer park ranger.

Jackson was quickly reminded that he belonged in the woods—much like where he grew up. He'd gone to the city because that was where his career led him, but he never fit in well with city life.

As a park ranger, Jackson enjoyed being outdoors. On duty, he checked in campers, cleaned the bathrooms, stocked the firewood, handled kayak rentals, and made sure the park ran smoothly. Off duty, he ran and explored the woods, taking in all that nature had to offer.

As soon as Jackson entered the ranger station after stowing his cleaning supplies in the storage shed, a smell hit him that nearly knocked him off his feet. Fresh strawberries, coconut, and vanilla. Not a combination you encounter often in the woods. Most of the smells he encountered in this building were stale body odors, either from long car rides or days without showers.

Marge, Jackson's fellow park ranger, was finishing up the paperwork for the campers in the minivan. She was the most unique person Jackson had ever met. Her husky but athletic build that almost took her to the Olympics for rugby was now perfect for her job as a ranger. Marge preferred to spend most of her time alone but was fiercely loyal to the few she called friends. Her love of jerky and caffeine was unmatched.

"What's that delicious smell? One of your fruity drinks?" Jackson asked. Marge was always trying the new flavors of energy drinks they came out with.

Marge quirked an eyebrow at him. "I don't know what smell you're talking about," she responded. "I haven't had anything but this crappy black coffee today."

What could smell so tantalizing? Jackson looked around, trying to follow the scent, and realized it led right out the door. Curiously, he asked Marge, "Who are our new campers?"

"Some young mom and her kids. She looked like she'd had a time of it getting here. They're in a tent on site 11. Hope she brought something to help her keep up with those balls of energy."

Jackson wanted to investigate the tempting scent that wouldn't leave his nostrils, but before he could take a step toward the door, the next two groups of campers entered. He helped Marge check them in and file the paperwork. After that, he had firewood to deliver to several sites, a toilet clog to deal with, a squabble to settle between two older men about what fish lived in the river, and a tree branch to clear off one of the hiking trails. By the time he had a moment to look for the source of the smell that had plastered a smile on his face all day, it was after dark.

Jackson closed up the station and walked over to site 11, following the fruity trail. Even in the dark, he could see a petite woman, curled up in her chair in front of a dying fire that was barely more than embers. Her gaze seemed far away and tears dried on her porcelain cheeks. Strawberries and coconut surrounded her so strongly that it propelled him forward. He didn't mean to startle her, but she didn't even glance up as he approached.

"Excuse me, miss," he said professionally. "It looks like you're having some trouble with your fire there. Mind if I take a look?"

The fire wasn't really what he wanted to look at. He wanted to memorize her every freckle, every strand of her strawberry-blonde hair that escaped the messy bun on top of her head. He couldn't wait to see her smile. Even in her sad, disheveled state, she was the most beautiful woman he'd ever laid eyes on. And then he saw it—the ring on her left hand.

She shifted her focus toward him but didn't say a word. He introduced himself as he began to build up her fire. She had tried but didn't have enough kindling to keep it going. Once the fire was built, he attempted one more time to get a response. "Are you here alone?"

"I—I'm sorry. You startled me. I'm here with my kids. They're asleep in the tent," Natalie responded, trying to compose herself.

"Would you like some company? I can show you how to keep your fire going," Jackson replied, trying not to seem too eager at the news that it was only children with her.

A woman with kids didn't bother him at all. A married woman, however, did. He didn't know the story of the missing man behind the ring on her finger, but he was going to find out.

Chapter Two

Natalie

Recovering from her shock, Natalie was finally able to fully take in the gorgeous man in front of her and answer him as if she wasn't in another world. "Okay," Natalie said timidly. She should have said, "No, thank you," but her mouth couldn't form the words. She also left out the fact that she'd known how to make a campfire since she was a teenager—she was just too tired and distracted this evening to care. The kids' chairs were too small for him, so Jackson took a seat on the bench of the picnic table.

"How old are your kids?"

"Noah is nine and Emma is five. And I'm Natalie. Natalie Evans. It's nice to meet you, Officer Lake."

"Please, call me Jackson. It's nice to meet you too, Natalie." Her name rolled smoothly off his lips. "Nine and five—I bet they're a handful. Will your husband be joining you?"

"We're separated. It's just me and the kids," she blurted. She didn't know what made her reveal such personal information to this stranger. A woman in her right mind would have told him her great bear of a husband was in the tent with the kids. Currently, she wasn't in her right mind. Something about this man made her trust him wholeheartedly and want to tell him everything.

They sat in silence for a while, stealing glances at each other and looking away when they made eye contact. Natalie finally broke the silence, wanting to hear his smooth voice again.

"How long have you been a ranger here?" she asked.

"Just a couple of months. I started in the spring when I needed a break from city life. The air here is said to heal the soul," Jackson answered.

His response resonated deep within Natalie. She'd planned for this to be a fun vacation. Somewhere along the way, their hearts and souls were broken by a man who seemed to have lost who he was. She wasn't sure there was enough air in the universe to heal what he broke, but this was a start.

"What made you decide to bring your kids camping by yourself?"

"We needed some soul-healing air," Natalie replied. She then proceeded to tell him everything.

Jackson

Jackson listened to every word of her story. How she planned the vacation with her husband, how he lost his job soon after, how he'd changed, how he'd requested separation and hadn't seen the kids since. Tears flowed freely down her cheeks and he longed to wipe them away.

"You know the saddest part?" Natalie asked rhetorically. Jackson didn't know what could be sadder than what she'd already shared. "I thought once he had a new job, it would fix our marriage—fix our family. But all it did was make him want to fix *me*." She laughed nervously before continuing, "He actually bought me a gym membership and hired a nanny without asking me—even told me I should think about starting botox. I'm twenty-nine. Who needs botox at twenty-nine?"

"Not you," Jackson let slip. "You're beautiful." Natalie's eyes went wide before she slipped into another sob.

Anger toward her husband simmered behind his eyes. Thankfully she couldn't see his expression in the dark. How could a man treat his wife and the mother of his children that way? She was perfect, but her husband clearly didn't see that.

Anger turned to confusion. Why did he feel so strongly about a woman he just met? A woman who was legally married. A woman who deserved more than to be left to care for her children alone. What was he getting himself into? He didn't know what drew him to her, but the pull was so strong, he knew there had to be greater forces at work.

As Natalie finished her story and grew quiet, the fire had dwindled back to embers. Jackson didn't want to say the wrong thing, like what a jerk her husband was, so instead he stood to leave. "It's getting late—you should get some sleep. The sun rises early here." He reached out his hand to help her stand. She hesitated before she took it, but when she did, lightning flowed through his fingers and one unexpected word echoed deep in his mind: *mine*.

Chapter Three

Natalie

What the crap was that? When Jackson had helped Natalie out of her chair, a shock ran through her body. After she was on her feet, he said good night and walked toward the ranger station. He didn't seem to notice anything strange.

Still confused by the entire interaction, she moved to her tent and opened it quietly. Both kids were sound asleep. The long car ride followed by all the running in the fresh air had worn them out. Natalie changed and cleaned her face with a wipe. She got in her sleeping bag and laid flat on her back, staring at the ceiling of the tent.

What is going on? She was supposed to be here to spend time with her kids and clear her head, not to meet a hot park ranger and divulge her whole life story in one night. Not to mention she was still married—she shouldn't be thinking about how hot another man was. But there was something about Jackson that made her heart pound and her head spin. She couldn't remember the last time Dave had given her so much as a flutter. In fact, he hadn't been intimate with her, or even touched her platonically, in quite some time.

Natalie lay in the dark, thoughts racing. Thinking about everything that had transpired, every little red flag that she should have caught in her marriage, every feeling she had ever felt, good or bad. She also thought about what she was feeling now, trying to sort out what exactly that was.

As she drifted off, she turned to her side. Through the wall of the tent, she thought she saw the silhouette of a wolf lying in the shadows of the nearby trees. But that wasn't possible. Wolves didn't live here.

Jackson

Walking away from Natalie that night was one of the hardest things Jackson had ever had to do. His feet felt like lead as he dragged them toward the ranger station. He needed to clear his head. He'd never felt this way about a woman.

Jackson wasn't inexperienced. He'd dated women, even had a few relationships. Nothing ever felt right. Nothing ever felt like this.

Instead of going into the building to grab his things and return to his rental cabin, he went behind the building and into the trees. He took off his boots and stuffed his socks inside. After stripping off his clothes, he stashed them behind a tree and shifted.

A huge silver-gray wolf with a white muzzle and four white paws took off running through the woods. Jackson wasn't able to spend a lot of time as a wolf in the city. Shifters weren't widely known among humans. He had to drive outside city limits to find somewhere to shift and run. On the weekends he wasn't on call, Jackson would sometimes return to his parents' apple orchard for family dinners. There, he could be himself and go for runs with his dad, but it wasn't the same as taking off whenever he wanted.

Here, he had the freedom he needed to run. The woods in this area were extensive and it didn't take him long to find areas away from humans where he could let his wolf free. Wolves were not a natural predator in this area, so being spotted by humans might cause some confusion.

Jackson stopped running. He hadn't even been paying attention to where he was. Right through those trees, Natalie was in her tent. His wolf had brought him to her, drawn to this woman he'd just met, who just happened to be unavailable. He couldn't bring himself to leave, so he crept just outside the trees and laid down, keeping watch. If he couldn't be with her, he would at least make sure she and her kids were protected.

As dawn started to peek through the trees, Jackson retreated into the woods. He had to retrieve his clothes and return to his cabin to shower before it was time for work.

Before she awoke, Jackson left Natalie a stack of firewood since they'd used up her small bundle last night. He placed some logs in her fire pit, ready to be lit for their morning breakfast if needed. Then he went to work.

Throughout the day, as he did his tasks, he couldn't help but glance toward site 11. In the morning, on the way to clean out the kayaks, he saw Natalie and the kids eating cereal. The children were beautiful, just as he expected. Noah was thin and a little short for his age, with auburn hair and his mother's blue eyes. He wore glasses that made him look smart, like he would be a doctor someday. Emma was the spitting image of her mother. Strawberry-blonde hair wild from sleep, freckles splattered on her nose and cheeks, and bright blue eyes filled with fire. If Jackson had to guess, she was a handful.

After the kayaks, Jackson checked the bathrooms and refilled the toilet paper. Then he took the golf cart around to the sites that had checked out and cleaned up any trash they left behind. When he got to the site across from Natalie's, he glanced over and saw her sitting between the two kids at the picnic table. She'd covered it with a tablecloth and they were coloring and chatting away.

Natalie was even more stunning in the daylight. Jackson couldn't look away. Even in cotton shorts, a faded T-shirt, and no makeup, she was radiant. Her hair was in a bun again, which he longed to set free. He wondered how long her tendrils would fall, how far he could run his fingers through them. Natalie looked up and caught him staring. She gave him a shy smile before looking back down at her work.

That little smile. It was just as magnificent as he imagined. Had she been fully smiling, she could have lit up the world. What was he going to do? He was already so far gone, he'd never be okay with letting her go.

Chapter Four

Natalie

Natalie felt a presence by her tent all night, but instead of keeping her awake, she slept like a log. She felt so safe, despite being alone with the kids in the woods. Maybe it was Officer Lake's presence that made her feel so protected. She'd never felt a connection like that with a man in such a short amount of time—or ever, for that matter. She was normally a very private person, keeping to herself and sharing only what she needed to. Something about Jackson made her lay it all out.

The first thing Natalie noticed when she left the tent the next morning was that her firewood was restocked. It made her smile, knowing someone had thought about her enough to bring her firewood. Dave hadn't done anything for her without being asked. Having him be the primary breadwinner had sounded great when they got engaged, but she didn't realize at the time that meant he would take no other responsibilities within their household.

After the long drive, Natalie decided to just hang out

around the campground with the kids and get settled today. After breakfast, they worked on one of her favorite things to do with the kids: crafts. They went to town on paper chains and lanterns. When they had made as many of those as they wanted, they colored in their favorite coloring books.

As her blue colored pencil moved across the page, she felt eyes on her and looked up from the picture she colored. Across the road was the most handsome park ranger. Seeing him in the daylight made her melt even more. He looked amazing in his green khaki cargo pants and tan camp shirt that stretched perfectly over his chest. She gave him a small smile, but then, feeling embarrassed for checking him out, went back to her coloring.

Natalie saw Jackson several more times throughout the day. After crafts, they walked over to the small playground and she took turns pushing the kids on the swings. Jackson's cart went by, loaded down with firewood, and she didn't miss when his gaze landed on her instead of the road.

When their stomachs started to grumble, Natalie and the kids returned to the campsite for a lunch of peanut butter and jelly sandwiches. She found herself frequently scanning the campground, searching for the alluring park ranger. She didn't know why she was so drawn to Jackson, but she couldn't seem to stop looking for him.

When they got down to the little beach along the river for an afternoon swim, Jackson was helping another couple get their kayaks in the water. He gave her a small wave, and a fire sparkled behind his eyes. She caught him watching as she played with the kids in the water—not in a creepy way, but with a look she couldn't quite place: admiration, or maybe longing. She found she wanted to know more about him. She wondered about his dreams, his ambitions, and his desires. After only one small conversation—one in which she talked more than listened—she was enamored by him in a way she'd never experienced so quickly before.

The kids swam and splashed, tried to catch minnows in a bucket, and built a sandcastle. After playing in the water for a while, Natalie sat on her towel, watching as the kids went swimming again after filling in the hole they spent ages digging. She hadn't been this relaxed in a long time.

She thought back to the last time the kids had been to the beach. Noah had been six and Emma was two. It was a hot summer day and the power had gone out after a thunderstorm the night before. She'd talked Dave into going with her to the beach at a nearby lake to cool down in the water. He spent the whole time on the phone with his office. How had she not seen then what she was starting to see now? That his job meant more than his family ever would.

When the sun started to set and the kids were thoroughly worn out, they went back to the campsite to cook hot dogs over the fire. Natalie hadn't seen her kids this happy in so long. Dave was always too busy working or schmoozing potential bosses to do anything with them, and until now, she was too nervous to do anything by herself. After today, she was starting to think she could do it herself...if it came to that.

As Natalie lit the fire that had already been built for her and got the hot dogs out of the cooler, a golf cart approached her site. She called out to the driver, "Officer Lake! Thank you for the fire, and the firewood. I really appreciate it."

"Please, call me Jackson. And it's no problem, really."

"Jackson, this is Noah and Emma," Natalie introduced. Turning to the kids, she said, "Kids, this is Jackson. He's the park ranger here. If you get in any trouble, you look for him or someone in this uniform, okay?"

"It's nice to meet you, kids. Are you enjoying your camping trip so far?"

"Yes, sir," Noah answered timidly, half hiding behind his mother.

"Will you eat hot dogs with us, Mr. Jackson? We're cooking them over the fire!" Emma nearly shouted. There was such a contrast between the quiet, reserved boy and the energetic social butterfly.

Jackson smiled at her and then smiled up at Natalie, whose cheeks were tinged with red. "If it's okay with your mom. I'm sure she didn't plan on feeding an extra person."

"Can he, Mom? Can he? We brought lots of hot dogs, right?" Emma asked.

Natalie nodded. Even her daughter took to the man immediately. Jackson walked over to the golf cart and grabbed a folding chair. They cooked their hot dogs and ate by the fire. The mood was much lighter than the previous night.

After hot dogs, they roasted some marshmallows and Jackson showed the kids how to turn them a nice golden brown. Natalie and Jackson laughed while the kids put on a puppet show with their toys that made no sense.

"Floopy and Lala were camping one day when an alien spaceship landed on their tent," Emma started, moving her stuffed animals along the picnic table.

"Out of the spaceship came an alien shark that could walk and breathe on land!" Noah continued. "The shark chased after Floopy and Lala, and tried to eat them."

"No, Noah," Emma whispered loudly. "The shark was their *friend*."

"But I want the shark to chase them," Noah argued.

Emma thought for a moment. "Okay, they can play tag. But the shark can't eat them. He doesn't have teeth."

"Fine." Noah gave a defeated sigh, giving into his little sister.

Jackson looked at Natalie with a raised brow and a goofy smile. Natalie just shrugged her shoulders while trying to hold back a laugh. The show ended with them singing a silly made-up song about a fish with legs in the woods. Natalie clapped and Jackson gave them a standing ovation.

"Sign them up for drama club. They'll be winning awards in no time," Jackson told Natalie.

"They do have good imaginations."

Jackson helped settle them down with a not-so-spooky ghost story before Natalie tucked them into bed.

Jackson

Jackson waited by the fire while Natalie went into her tent with the kids. Once the kids were settled down, Natalie dropped into her chair next to Jackson. She sat in silence for a while, watching the fire, while Jackson watched her. The light from the flames flickering across her face kept him mesmerized. He finally broke the silence when his staring risked becoming awkward. "The kids seem to be having a good time."

"Yeah. They are. It's been a long time since I've seen them so happy and...free." Natalie paused thoughtfully while fidgeting with the hem of her shirt. "Listen, I'm sorry about last night. I didn't mean to dump all that on you when we just met. I just...had a long day and I haven't had a chance to process everything."

"It's no problem, really. I'm here anytime you need to get anything off your chest." He immediately regretted his choice of words, as it led him to think about all the things *he'd* like to get off her chest. He hoped she didn't notice as he had to adjust his belt and his eyes took on a green glow.

"I didn't get a chance to ask anything about you. You said you came here to escape the city. What did you do there?" Natalie asked. She turned her gaze toward Jackson as she awaited his response.

"I'm a veterinarian. I worked as an assistant in a large clinic until the owner got involved with some shady billing practices. I decided then it was time to take a break from the city and ended up here."

The lighthearted conversation continued from there. "Is your family in the city?" Natalie questioned.

"No, I was the only family member to venture that far away from the apple orchard where I grew up. My mom, dad, two brothers, and two sisters all still live in my hometown." A pain of longing hit him briefly. It had been too long since he'd seen his family.

"Wow, four siblings? I can't even imagine," Natalie replied. "I'm an only child. I always wanted brothers and sisters, but my mom, Kathryn, died when I was young and my dad never remarried. The closest thing I had was my nanny, Eloise."

"I'm sorry about your mom. That had to have been hard. Were you close to your dad?" Jackson asked.

Natalie scoffed. "Sorry. Robert is a corporate lawyer. I saw him about as much as my kids have seen their father lately. I spent most of my time with Eloise, or with my grandparents." Natalie shook her head. "Now that I think about it, I should have known better than to marry someone with corporate ambitions."

Jackson bristled at the mention of her husband but, not wanting to darken the conversation, tried to move away from that point of contention. "Being the oldest of five, there are times I would have given anything to be an only child. Especially when my sisters would get after me about how I dressed or did my hair. They were always trying to set me up with any pretty girl they came across."

Natalie giggled. "I doubt you needed any help in that department."

"You'd be surprised," Jackson teased. "None of the girls they found were ever as pretty as you, though." He knew he shouldn't be flirting with a married woman, but with Natalie, he couldn't help himself. The way she lit up when he complimented her only made him want to do it more.

"Jackson, I'm sure that's not true."

"It is true. How about you? I bet you couldn't keep the boys away."

"Not true at all. I was super shy, and then I married Dave just after I turned nineteen, so there weren't a lot of boys."

Jackson stood to add another log to the fire, unsure of how to respond. He knew Natalie was trying to process all that was going on with her husband, but every mention of the guy made him want to leave immediately to hunt the jerk down. Natalie was so sweet, and such a good mom—she didn't deserve to be treated like anything less. If talking to him would help her, he would listen to every word, as painful as it may be.

"Well, we've covered work, family, and our sad love

lives. How about friends?" Jackson asked when he returned to his chair.

"Most of my friends drifted away after high school when they went to college and I didn't."

Natalie shifted in her chair uncomfortably. Jackson was becoming hyper aware of her every movement—her every breath.

"In fact, the best thing to come out of this whole situation is Lacey, my nanny," Natalie continued. "Dave hired her to watch the kids when he thought I should be at the gym, but we spent most of our time together. We had so much in common, from our coffee order to our favorite books, it didn't take long for us to be best friends."

"She sounds like a wonderful friend." Jackson was glad Natalie had someone to talk to. She'd been through so much and he didn't like that she didn't have a family to support her.

"She is. What about your friends? Are they living it up in the city while you're roughing it in the woods?"

Jackson shook his head. "No, no. They worked me pretty hard at the clinic so I didn't have a lot of time to make friends. My brothers are my best friends. Even though they're quite a bit younger, we're still really close. Especially Travis. My coworker, Marge, has become a good friend too."

"Marge? The ranger who checked us in?" Natalie questioned, a hint of something resembling jealousy in her voice.

"That's her. She's been here for years. I think you'd like her."

"Oh. I hope I get the chance to know her better, since she's your friend."

They talked until the fire burned to only coals, having once again gone through all the wood Jackson had brought.

He'd have to bring a bigger stack tomorrow. He didn't like his time with her being cut short. He told Natalie good night, his eyes lingering as she retreated into her tent. As she turned to close the zipper on the tent, he caught a smoldering look in her eyes. Just like the night before, a word echoed in his mind. This time it was louder and closer to the surface. This time it said *mate*.

Jackson took the cart back to the station, leaving his chair, knowing he'd be back. He grabbed his keys, hopped in his truck, and drove home. His thoughts wandered. *The Wolf Prince*, a story his father told him as a child, filtered into his mind.

One day, the prince was out for a walk when he picked up a strong new scent in the woods. He searched for the flowers that could produce such a scent, for it must be thousands of them. It smelled like honeysuckle and jasmine. When he got to the source of the smell, he didn't find flowers at all, but a beautiful girl.

It couldn't be possible—could it? The lore of fated mates having a uniquely strong smell that only their mate could recognize was passed on for generations. It was said that each shifter had a mate, and the connection between them was instant and could never be broken. Jackson's dad would tell him the story of the wolf prince and, later, of how he met his own mate, Jackson's mother.

Sitting on a boulder by the stream, the girl with long blonde hair was crying. She was lost in the woods and couldn't find her way home. As the prince approached her, she looked into his eyes and a voice whispered in the back of his mind, telling him that this was his mate. His perfect princess. The prince offered the girl his hand and he felt sparks at her touch.

As a teenager, Jackson dreamed of finding his "perfect

princess," that one person who could accept what he was and love him unconditionally. As he entered his thirties, he wondered if it was true or if it was just a bedtime story made up by his dad. Here now with Natalie, the story replayed in his head and he began to believe once again. The scent that surrounded her, the constant pull he felt toward her, the way that in just over twenty-four hours she had taken over all his thoughts—it all fit. The words echoed in his mind again. *Mate. Mine.*

He'd taken the job as a ranger to get some clarity on his future, but now it was even more muddled than before. He had a mate, and she was here with her little family. He had a strong, beautiful mate, who was married. Separated, but married nonetheless. Why were the fates so cruel?

He should just walk away. He wasn't interested in being a homewrecker. There could be a chance she wanted to reconcile with her husband—she said they had been together for ten years, after all. His wolf let out a growl at that thought. The mate bond was unbreakable and irreplaceable. If he didn't win her over, he would be alone forever. And if all the lore was true, he would suffer immeasurable pain as a result.

He fell on his bed, fully clothed, staring up at the ceiling. He couldn't stop thinking about this woman who was taking up space rent-free in his head. He undid his belt, letting free his hardness that had been growing increasingly more uncomfortable. He took a cold shower, getting used to the idea that he'd be taking a lot of them, but when his wolf wouldn't settle, he found himself running through the woods toward the campground on four legs.

Chapter Five

Natalie

When Natalie awoke, she was disappointed to see a female ranger, seemingly in her mid-thirties, unloading a stack of wood at her site. Her dirty blonde hair was pulled into a short ponytail and tucked through the gap in her ranger cap to keep it out of the way as she worked. Natalie thought the ranger was pretty in a strong and very tall way. She wondered if she was the type of woman Jackson went for. *Where did that thought come from?*

"Good morning," Natalie said politely.

"Mornin'. Officer Lake asked me to drop off some wood for you."

"Thank you very much, ma'am."

"I'm no ma'am. The name's Marge."

"Thank you, Marge."

Marge finished unloading the large load of wood without breaking a sweat. Natalie marveled at how she'd done it so effortlessly. She had gotten stronger with her scheduled gym trips, but she still struggled with one bundle, let alone a whole truckload.

When she finished, Marge turned back to her truck. Natalie thought about last night and about the wolf silhouette she thought she'd seen for a second time. She called out, "Marge, can I ask you a question?"

"Sure. What's that?"

"Are there wolves around here?"

Marge looked surprised at first, but then answered with a grin, "Wolves? No. There might be a few coyotes. Maybe a black bear or two. But I've never heard of there being any wolves." Marge got in the truck and drove to the station.

Maybe it was a coyote outside her tent, but it seemed awfully big for a coyote. *And why would a coyote be sleeping outside my tent? Why would a wolf?* Natalie shook her head. Maybe she didn't know what she saw. Or maybe she was losing her mind. With all she had going on, it was a valid option.

Before she could think about it anymore, the kids came out of the tent looking for their breakfast. After another day of cereal, Natalie and the kids dressed and packed for a hike. They couldn't go far before Emma's legs would get tired, but there was a mile-and-a-half loop around one of the waterfalls that she could handle.

The landscape was beautiful. The campground was near the mouth of the river, which went on for miles and miles, and over several waterfalls. On the other side of the river was a meadow of wildflowers where deer, elk, and other animals would come for a drink.

The trail led them through the woods and up behind one of the waterfalls. They saw squirrels and chipmunks, along with birds of all different kinds. At one point, Natalie had a moment of panic when Emma shrieked.

"It's only a snake, Em," Noah said as he grabbed it by the tail and dangled it in front of her, which made her shriek even more.

Natalie gasped. "Noah, please *put that down*."

Noah put the snake down, but not without rolling his eyes. "It was just a snake, Mom."

Natalie was starting to see subtle changes in her normally sweet boy. She hoped it was just that he was nearing his preteen years, and that it didn't have anything to do with the situation with his father. She chose to ignore the eye roll this time and continue walking.

"There are lots of different snakes here, Noah. Not like the ones we see in the park. There are even some that are venomous. When we're out in nature like this, we need to let nature be. We can look with our eyes, or our cameras, but we shouldn't touch."

"Can we touch wolves, Momma?" Emma asked.

Natalie froze in place. "No. You absolutely cannot touch wolves. Why would you ask that?"

Emma shrugged. "I heard you ask that lady if there are wolves here. I thought maybe if we saw one, we could pet it, since they are kind of like dogs."

What is it with this place and wolves? "Wolves may look like dogs, but they are very dangerous. I don't think you have to worry about getting close enough to touch one, anyway." Natalie didn't quite believe the words coming out of her own mouth, thinking of the proximity of their tent to the tree line.

They crossed a suspension bridge over the river and started their descent along the other side. As they walked downhill, they started to hear the rushing of the waterfall. When they got to the bottom, there was a boardwalk overlooking the falls where tourists could stop and take their pictures, built with the hopes that it would keep them from wandering off the trail to get a better look. Natalie and the kids had the spot to themselves. They sat on a bench to eat protein bars and drink some water while they watched the falls.

"When you've finished your snacks, let's get some pictures," Natalie told them as they wrapped up. "Scoot over there by the fence."

Natalie nudged the kids over where she wanted them, and that's when she saw it: a dark gray wolf stood at the top of the falls, drinking from the river. Its black muzzle contrasted with the clear water as it lifted its head to examine its surroundings. Natalie's eyes went wide when it made eye contact with her. When she finally thought to snap a picture, it was gone. She closed her eyes and shook her head, trying to clear what she thought must have been a daydream. Marge had said there weren't any wolves here.

Natalie quickly got a few pictures of the kids and then they continued on their way back to camp. While they ate their sandwiches for lunch, Natalie took in how filthy they all were. She rounded up supplies and herded the kids toward the showers. She watched expectantly as she walked, but didn't see Jackson anywhere. She hadn't seen him all day. She didn't know why she expected him to be around, but she did.

Noah handled his shower and Natalie went in with Emma to help her. She did her best to wash down what she could of her own body with a soapy washcloth. When they were finished, they were on their way to the campsite when a certain park ranger came up beside them.

Jackson

Jackson needed some space. Being so near to Natalie without being able to hold her, touch her, or kiss her was torture. He barely knew this woman and yet his feelings toward her were stronger than anything he'd ever experienced. While he was enjoying getting to know her and the kids, he wanted to get to know her in all the ways only a mate could. He didn't think he was going to be able to resist much longer. Proximity made it even harder. So when he left his guard post at the first signs of dawn, he ran to his cabin.

His shift didn't start for several hours and Jackson had been spending more time at the campground than usual, so he used the extra time to catch up on chores. He threw in a load of laundry, had some breakfast, did up the dishes, and took out the trash—the whole time thinking about his beautiful mate. He thought about the way her eyes sparkled when she was with her kids. The way she opted for comfort over the latest styles that made no sense for camping but were often worn by young female campers anyway. The way she didn't wear makeup and kept her hair up to maximize her time with her children. The way she blushed anytime he caught her looking at him. Jackson opted for another cold shower before heading to work.

He knew he couldn't avoid Natalie forever, nor did he want to. He didn't want to avoid her at all, but before he could see her again, he needed to regain his sense of self-control. He couldn't risk running to her and taking things way too far.

When Jackson got to the ranger station, Marge was already there, making coffee. She had a very woodsy smell that Jackson attributed to her job; however, there was something about it that was oddly unique but familiar. "Hey, Marge, could you do me a favor and deliver a few bundles of firewood to site 11? I already loaded them in the truck."

"Why can't you deliver it? Isn't managing wood your favorite job?" Marge snickered.

"I just—please, Marge. I'll get you a Starbucks next time I go on a supply run."

"Oh, fine. You do know my love language," she grumbled as she went out the door. Jackson looked for something to keep himself busy. He and Marge made a good team, so there was very little paperwork to catch up on.

The campground would close for the season soon and his temporary position would end. Jackson decided it was time to start thinking about what came next. He wasn't going back to the city, that much he knew. He pulled up his resume and started looking for small-town veterinary clinics to apply to, starting with his hometown.

By lunch he'd sent out a few resumes, tidied up the office, and gotten the paperwork ready for the incoming campers. After being in the station all morning, he needed some fresh air and to stretch his legs. He headed over for a bathroom check when he saw a familiar messy bun walking beside what appeared to be a large yellow duck.

As soon as he saw Natalie, space seemed like the last thing he needed. His legs didn't feel like his own as Jackson quickly caught up to them just as a small pair of feet tripped over the duck towel. He quickly caught Emma before she fell. "Careful there, little duck!"

Emma looked startled at first until she registered who had caught her. "Mr. Jackson! Guess what? We went on a hike today and we saw a waterfall and squirrels and birds and a snake." Emma rattled off her list so fast and with such increasing speed and volume that she was almost incoherent until she shouted, "And we saw a wolf!"

Both Jackson and Natalie's heads snapped toward the girl. "A wolf?" Jackson asked.

"A big gray wolf at the top of the waterfall! It was taking a drink and then it looked at us and then ran away. It was so cute!" Emma was so observant sometimes, it was scary.

Natalie looked deep in thought. "I didn't know she saw it, too," she said quietly.

Jackson started to panic. Had he been seen? *No, dummy. You were in the office all morning and nowhere near the waterfall.* "What did the wolf look like? Are you sure it wasn't a dog or a coyote?"

Natalie shook her head. "I'm sure. It was much too big to be a coyote. It was dark gray with a black muzzle. I went to take a picture but it was gone. I thought maybe I imagined it, but if Emma saw it too..." Natalie trailed off.

"Hmm. There haven't been any wolf sightings around here before. I'll have to investigate. Let me know if you see it again. We may have to contact Fish and Wildlife."

Natalie looked like she wanted to say something else. Her lips parted, but no words came out. She closed them again and looked down at her feet. She was hiding something.

"What are your plans for the rest of the day?" Jackson asked, changing the subject.

"Nothing too dirty, hopefully," Natalie said with a smile. "I'd love a shower but I can't leave these two alone."

Nothing dirty was the exact opposite of what he'd like to be doing with her. His thoughts about her were getting feral as the desire to claim his mate grew stronger every minute that he was with her. She was so gorgeous, on top of being an amazing mom. She would sacrifice everything for her kids. Jackson wondered if anyone had ever sacrificed anything for her.

"Why don't you go ahead and get your things? I can watch them for a few minutes." Babysitting campers wasn't usually a part of Jackson's job description, but if his mate needed a shower, he'd make sure she got one—along with anything else she needed.

A wrinkle formed between her brows as she thought about his request. He worried she wouldn't trust leaving her kids with him, but after a moment she responded, "Really? If you're sure. That would be so amazing. Just a quick one."

"Of course. Go get clean. We'll be right here." Jackson loved how she lit up at the idea of a shower. He wondered if she'd light up the same way at the idea of a shower with him. He couldn't think about that now.

"Let's get these towels hung up while your mom gets a shower," Jackson said to the kids as he led them over to the clothesline tied between the trees.

Chapter Six

Natalie

Natalie probably should have thought twice about leaving her kids with someone she just met, but she was desperate for a shower. Besides, he was a park employee—if anyone could be trusted, he could. The odd thing was, she did trust him, fully and completely. A trust she didn't have with Dave. She hadn't ever left him alone with the kids.

When Noah was a baby, Dave had agreed to watch him while Natalie went to the grocery store. She was gone for an hour, and even after leaving specific instructions, came back to a crying baby, a dirty diaper, and two percent milk in the bottle. From then on, she took them with her wherever she went and even made sure to shower while they were asleep. She couldn't remember another time when Dave had been alone with them, or had even offered to give her time to herself. When he did give her time, it was for activities of his choosing—and he called the nanny.

As she stood under the hot water, Natalie's thoughts

drifted to Jackson. He'd rarely left her mind since they met. She enjoyed talking to him. In contrast to Dave, he genuinely liked to learn about her and he listened to what she had to say. He didn't seem to enjoy talking about himself, almost as if he were holding back. And those eyes, as green as the trees that surrounded them—she could spend the rest of her life looking in those eyes. She'd never seen eyes that seemed to glow, especially when they looked at her. They were almost...animalistic.

Aside from his eyes, she longed to see (and feel) the lines of his muscles that pressed against his shirt. She also wondered about what was so snugly packed in the belt he kept adjusting. He tried to be discreet but he didn't know she saw him—every time. Natalie tried to shake the thoughts out of her head as she felt them in her core. They made her feel like some sexual predator waiting to strike.

Thinking about predators made her think about the wolf. Natalie had been shocked when Emma said she'd seen it too. She hadn't said anything to the kids at the time and they didn't mention it, either. At least that confirmed that it wasn't part of her imagination. Jackson didn't act like she was crazy, either. She had wanted to tell him about the wolf shadow outside her tent, but she wasn't entirely sure *that* wasn't in her imagination. Imaginary or not, it gave her a sense of security. The same way she felt when Jackson was around.

Natalie finished her shower and got dressed in a clean pair of shorts and a novelty tank. Her kids loved it when she wore their favorite characters. Some of them were her favorites, too. She combed through her hair and added some mousse, scrunching in her curls. She'd leave it down to air dry and put it in her signature bun later. She didn't like to spend a lot of time on her hair unless she was going out somewhere, which she rarely ever did.

Natalie was almost to the campsite when she stopped in her tracks, not believing what she saw. Jackson was on all fours, Emma on his back growling and laughing. They were chasing a prancing Noah, who held sticks up to his head like antlers. She stood and watched as they chased him around and around in circles, until Noah tripped. Natalie sharply sucked in a breath, worried he might be hurt, but he caught himself and gently lowered to the ground and rolled over. Jackson and Emma pounced and began tickling Noah until they were all rolling around and laughing. So much for not getting dirty.

At that moment, Natalie realized the dirt didn't matter. The kids had never played like this with their father. If they played so wildly, he would have been snapping at them to be quiet and sending them to their rooms. Doubts swirled in her mind. She'd been fighting to keep her family together for months. She did what Dave asked, not because she was afraid of him—he had never harmed her—but because if she didn't, they would argue. She didn't like to argue in front of the kids. She wanted them to see parents who got along, parents who worked together as a cohesive unit, and parents who loved them and each other.

In trying to keep things together, Natalie had been oblivious to all they were missing. Her children didn't see affectionate parents. They didn't see parents who worked together to manage the household. They didn't see a father who supported their mother. They didn't see a father who supported *them*. Tears threatened to escape her eyes, though she didn't know if they were happy or sad. She had shed so many already on this trip.

Natalie was holding back with Jackson because even

though Dave asked for this separation, she still had taken vows. She wouldn't be the one to break them, although she had suspicions that Dave could have broken them already. She wouldn't cheat, even if he had, but maybe letting Jackson in as a friend would be okay. They were only here for a few more days, anyway—it wouldn't hurt for Natalie and the kids to have some fun.

Jackson

Jackson tapped into his inner child, playing wolves and deer with the kids. Their laughs filled the air. It was a sound he hoped filled his own home someday. As they rolled in the dirt, tickling and laughing, Jackson was feeling a tinge of guilt at getting the kids messy again. When a recognizable scent drifted on the breeze, he got to his feet, eyes blazing.

Natalie's scent was stronger when she was fresh from the shower. He even thought he smelled a hint of her arousal, but it was tainted with the salty scent of tears. Her hair was finally down and he admired the long springy curls. As he moved toward her, he reached out to pull one of the curls and let it bounce back into place. "You're beautiful," he stated, gazing into those blue eyes that grew brighter by the day. Natalie looked away shyly, a rosy flush spreading over her cheeks. Discomfort showed in her demeanor, revealing that she wasn't used to receiving such compliments. Jackson was going to change that.

Checking his watch, Jackson had an idea. "My shift is over in an hour. Can I take you and the kids kayaking? There are some amazing views I'd love to show you." *Nothing as amazing as my view right now, though.*

"That sounds like fun," Natalie replied quickly, sending a smile beaming across Jackson's face.

"Good. Can you pack a picnic dinner and meet me at the beach in an hour?"

"Sure. Sounds good." A smile that mirrored his own grew on Natalie's lips, and it was just as incredible as he imagined.

Jackson went to do his bathroom check and finish up his work in the office, all with the same big smile plastered on his face. Her quick reply and the smile on her face gave him hope that Natalie was just as eager to spend time with him as he was with her.

"You sure are happy these days. Anything you want to share with the class?" Marge asked when he entered the office.

Not knowing what else to say, Jackson replied, "I met someone."

"Site 11?" Marge questioned without looking up from her crossword puzzle.

"How did you know?"

Marge paused. Jackson thought he saw her sniff the air and give a small shake of her head. "Because you're always here, and the only other campers are fishermen or couples."

Jackson realized she was right. There weren't any other families or young women camped here at the moment. "It's complicated. We're just getting to know each other."

"Natalie seems nice, but didn't I see a ring on her finger?"

"Like I said, it's complicated." Jackson didn't like where

this conversation was going. He didn't want to think about the dirtbag keeping him from his mate. "I want to take her hiking on the West Trail Friday evening to see the sunset over the Upper Falls. It's too far for the kids. Can they hang out with you for a while?"

"Uh, what am I going to do with kids?"

"I don't know. Drive them around in the golf cart. Play cards. Feed them some marshmallows. Please, Marge? I'll owe you big time."

"Fine. You better make that Starbucks a venti. And add some cake pops."

"You got it, Marge. Thanks!" Jackson finished his shift and left for the beach. He pulled out two double kayaks, paddles, and lifejackets. He had it all set up when Natalie and the kids arrived.

Chapter Seven

Natalie

Natalie couldn't look away as she strolled to the beach. The muscles on Jackson's bare chest rippled, moving flawlessly under his tanned skin, as he prepared the kayaks. His body was not afraid of hard work, and it showed. That physique couldn't be manufactured in a gym.

Natalie had put the kids in their swimsuits, knowing she wouldn't be able to keep them out of the water. She wore a one-piece suit under her nylon shorts. She wasn't a bikini girl. She was too ashamed of the stretch marks and scars that were souvenirs left by her beautiful babies.

Jackson had life jackets laid out for each of them. "Have you kayaked before?" he asked as she got the kids all snapped in and got into the purple kayak with Noah.

"I have, a long time ago, but this will be a first for the kids," Natalie responded. Her grandparents had a kayak that she would paddle around the small lake by their house when she visited in the summer.

Jackson took Emma in the green kayak and showed

them how to paddle properly. Noah would be able to paddle a little, but Emma wouldn't be much help. They entered the water and started paddling up the river. While they moved at a leisurely pace, Jackson told them funny stories of campers he had before them.

"Kayaks are pretty hard to tip. But my first week here, a couple of college kids were out celebrating the end of the semester. One of the guys dropped his paddle and leaned over the side to reach for it, just as his friend decided it would be a good idea to stand up."

"What happened?" Noah asked.

Jackson chuckled. "They rolled their boat right over. Dumped all their stuff and came back soaked. One of them was even missing a shoe."

The kids laughed, while Natalie shouted, "Got that, kids? No leaning, no standing!"

"Just last week, a couple came back and swore they saw Bigfoot."

It was Emma's turn to ask, "What's a Bigfoot?"

"A tall, hairy monster that people often claim to see in the woods," Jackson answered.

"But Mommy says monsters aren't real."

"Your mommy is a smart lady," Jackson said. "They didn't see any monsters. Just a pigeon hunter in a grass camouflage suit."

"A pigeon hunter? Why on earth would anyone hunt pigeons?" Natalie questioned with a confused look on her face.

"I really don't know," Jackson answered with a huge grin and a shake of his head. The way he responded made them all laugh.

Talking about hunters made Natalie think about the wolf at the waterfall. She was suddenly concerned for its safety, despite it being an apex predator. "Are there a lot of hunters here?" she asked Jackson.

"Not this time of year. The campground is closed for most hunting seasons."

A wave of relief washed over Natalie. She didn't know why a random wolf's well-being meant so much to her, but knowing there weren't a bunch of men with guns in the woods did give her comfort.

They continued to move up the river. When Emma tried to paddle, she sent a spray of water toward Noah. In return, he smacked his paddle, trying to send a splash toward his sister but hitting Jackson instead. Soon they were all splashing and laughing, having a great time.

Natalie let loose a playfulness she had tamped down for years. When Jackson smiled at her, water dripping down his bare chest, a mischievous grin spread across her face. She raised her eyebrows at him and shouted, "Race you!" taking off up the river as fast as she could. Noah paddled furiously along with Natalie, but Jackson quickly overtook them. Emma's little arms moved as fast as they would go but her paddle barely touched the water. When Jackson started to turn the next bend in the river, Natalie called out, "Okay, okay. You win."

Jackson slowed and called to her, "We're almost there." He led them to a clearing where they pulled out the kayaks and had their picnic. Natalie had prepared a stack of sandwiches, bags of chips, grapes, and a package of cookies. They watched a deer get a drink across the river and fish jumping along the riverbank. Emma squealed gleefully when a beaver slapped its tail. The kids were loving every minute of it.

Jackson sat close to Natalie, watching the kids splash in the water after they ate. Not close enough to touch but close enough that she could smell the cedar and evergreen cologne he wore, much like the trees that surrounded them. The looks they shared were filled with an array of emotions: attraction, joy, confusion, guilt, understanding, sadness, longing, and something else she couldn't put a word to.

Conflict warred in her mind. *Dave left me. Why shouldn't I be with Jackson? Because I'm still married, that's why. Dave is probably shacked up with some supermodel blonde. Jackson probably doesn't want me anyway; he's just being nice. Is it normal for park rangers to take campers kayaking if they're just being nice? We're only here a couple more days—how would Dave even know? I can't risk the kids getting attached, but oh, how good would it feel to be in his strong arms? It won't feel so good when it's time to leave.*

"What's going on in that pretty head of yours?" Jackson asked as he leaned back on his elbows, pulling Natalie from her thoughts.

"Just thinking," Natalie responded. If only she could tell him what about.

"You looked happy today."

"This was great. Thank you for bringing us. I wouldn't have been brave enough to do it myself." Natalie was learning that she could do a lot of things on her own, but she didn't think kayaking was one of them. "Dave would have hated this," Natalie mumbled under her breath.

"Why go camping if he didn't like it?"

Natalie didn't answer at first. She didn't think she had spoken loud enough for Jackson to hear her. She must have been louder than she thought. Hugging her knees, she responded, "I spent a lot of time with my grandparents during the summer while my dad worked. They lived on a lake and I spent most of my time there outdoors. My kids have never seen anything but the city. I wanted them to experience the serenity and joy that the outdoors could bring."

Natalie paused, deep in thought. Her eyes drifted over the water as she began, almost speaking to herself. "Now that I think about it, Dave probably wasn't even listening when he agreed to come. Any other time I suggested we take the kids somewhere, he made some excuse as to why he couldn't take time off. I was so excited he agreed to this trip, but he probably didn't even know what he was agreeing to. A week later, he lost his job and everything changed."

Their silence resumed as they watched the kids play, but Natalie's mind was somewhere else. She thought of her months of pinching pennies while Dave searched for a new job. The longer Dave went without a job, the more depressed he became. He was always agitated, his anger igniting at the smallest inconvenience, and everything that went wrong became Natalie's fault. She should have seen then that the relationship they once had was gone. One look at Jackson and she knew that her relationship with Dave at its best was nothing like this non-relationship. *Did Dave really change, or was I just too blind to see how he was before?*

As dusk approached, they got in the kayaks and paddled down the river. After reaching the beach, Jackson walked with Natalie as the kids ran ahead in their own little world. Their hands brushed as they walked without saying a word and the smallest of sparks passed between them. When they got to the campsite, Natalie sent the kids to get ready for bed.

"Thanks for today. I had a lot of fun," Natalie told Jackson.

"I'm glad you enjoyed it." So many unsaid things lingered between them. "Friday is my day off. If you're not busy in the afternoon, would you like to go for a hike with me?"

"I'd like to, but what about the kids?"

"They can stay with Marge. They'll get a kick out of her. She's completely safe and has already agreed to hang out with them."

Natalie thought about it. She should say no. Leaving her kids long enough for a shower close by was one thing, but leaving them with someone she just met while she went on a long hike made her nervous. On top of that, with all the feelings flowing through her, she didn't trust herself to be alone with the alluring park ranger. However, she wanted nothing more than to spend more time with him, and she believed him when he said the kids would be okay with Marge. Park rangers were essentially the police of the parks, anyway.

"Okay, let's plan on it." Her heart pounded at the thought of being alone in the woods with Jackson. He smiled and said good night, leaving her in anticipation.

Jackson

It was getting harder and harder for Jackson to keep his distance from Natalie. He wanted to touch her, hold her, kiss her. He wanted to stroke her hair while they sat and watched the kids play. He wanted to take away all the pain her husband caused her. He wanted to hold her hand as they walked, to follow her into her tent and hold her through the night.

The pull to be with his mate was getting stronger, and he didn't know how much longer he'd be able to restrain himself. Natalie only had a couple more days of her vacation left, and then what? How could he keep himself from following her back to the husband who didn't seem to want her but wouldn't fully let her go?

Jackson reluctantly drove to his cabin. He loved Natalie's little picnic, but it was nowhere near enough for a wolf. He threw a steak on the grill and grabbed his phone. He pulled up his contact list and made a call to the first person on his favorites.

"Hi, Dad," Jackson said solemnly when his dad picked up the phone.

"Jackson! How are you, son? You sound troubled." Jackson was glad to hear his father's voice. He knew if anyone would know what to do, it would be him.

A heavy pause hung in the air while Jackson tried to find the words to admit why he'd called. "I've found my mate." He sighed.

"That's wonderful! When can we meet her? Before the wedding, I hope."

"It's...complicated, Dad. She's married with two young children." Jackson flipped his steak and went into the house for a plate.

"Well, that does complicate things. Are you sure she's your mate?"

"Positive. Her smell is...and I can't...I can't stay away. Dad, what do I do? She's separated from her husband, but they're still legally married. She's here camping with her kids on her own and will only be here a couple more days." Jackson told him all about the time they'd spent together—

how much he enjoyed spending time with her and the kids, how gorgeous she was, how sweet Emma looked just like her, and how he'd watched Noah slowly coming out of his shell. "I just want to be near her all the time. I don't know what I'm going to do when she leaves."

"Fate has its ways, but one thing's for certain—the mate bond is unbreakable. You will forever be connected. If you can't be her mate, you'll have to settle for being whatever it is she needs you to be."

"How do I do that without crossing the line? The pull is so strong." Turning off the grill, Jackson plated the meat, but he wasn't sure he had an appetite anymore.

Jackson's dad didn't respond right away. Jackson waited, knowing there was no easy answer. "I never had to resist the pull with your mother. Maybe find another outlet, somewhere to let out your...frustrations." Jackson saw more running and cold showers in his future.

"Thanks, Dad." Jackson was ready to say goodbye when he remembered what Emma had talked about earlier. The wolf. "Have you heard about any shifters in this area? Natalie thinks she saw a wolf at the waterfall. Emma saw it too. This isn't their natural habitat, so if it's a shifter, they need to be more careful."

"No, I haven't heard of wolves there in quite some time. Might be a rogue shifter. Stay alert."

"Bye, Dad."

"Take care, son. And remember: Fate has her reasons for everything. There's a reason she gave you Natalie."

The call had given Jackson lots to think about. He was going to have to find a way to ignore the temptation to claim his mate in as many different ways as he could. He wanted to claim every inch of her body. He wanted to claim her heart. He wanted to replace that too-small ring on her finger and raise her children alongside her, as if they were his own. He never wanted to see her sad or hurting again. Ultimately, he just wanted to see her happy. If that meant sending her back to her husband, that's what he would have to do.

As for the wolf, a rogue shifter could be trouble. He'd never met one but his dad had told him stories. Rogues could be unpredictable. Some had trouble adjusting to being a wolf. Some gave in a little too fully to the wolf inside. Jackson would need to investigate carefully. He couldn't have a rogue around his mate. He finished his steak, stripped off his clothes, shifted, and took his place outside Natalie's tent.

Chapter Eight

Natalie

The next morning, Natalie and the kids drove out to the nearby town. She needed to get a few groceries for the remainder of the trip and thought the kids might like to visit some of the shops. Tired of cereal, they started with breakfast at the local diner.

Natalie and the kids walked in through the diner entrance and took in their surroundings. Mirroring the woodsy atmosphere outside, the diner had a very rustic feel. The log walls were covered with photos and certificates from local fishing and hunting competitions. Behind the counter were various mounted fish and small animals. While Emma and Noah pointed out the different animals, a hostess approached her podium and began selecting menus and utensils. Before the hostess could seat them, however, Natalie's head spun across the diner and her gaze landed on a familiar face.

Jackson sat in a booth along the windows, and when she caught his eye, his face lit up with a smile. He gave them a beckoning wave that indicated they should join him. Natalie's pulse jumped in excitement at the opportunity to spend more time with him. She still didn't understand the magnetic pull she felt toward Jackson, and still felt guilty for the feelings that continued to grow—but the guilt lessened as more revelations of her failing marriage came to the surface.

After asking the hostess if they could sit with their friend, Natalie walked the kids over and slid into the booth across from Jackson with a kid on either side.

"Good morning, little duck," Jackson said to Emma. She smiled from ear to ear. Emma loved Jackson's nickname for her.

To Noah, he nodded and raised an eyebrow in question. "Champ?"

Noah smiled and nodded back.

Finally, Jackson looked at Natalie. "And good morning to you too, beautiful."

Natalie felt her cheeks heat. She didn't think she'd ever get used to being called beautiful. "Good morning, Jackson. I didn't expect to see you here."

"Well, Marge may like her Starbucks, but it's this place that has the best coffee. The pancakes aren't bad, either," he said with a wink toward the kids.

A waitress took their drink order while they looked at the menu. When their drinks arrived, Natalie ordered a ham and cheese omelet. With Natalie's permission, Jackson ordered the kids' menu special for each of the children—pancakes with sprinkles topped with whipped cream and a cherry, otherwise known as *party pancakes*. For himself, Jackson ordered the big breakfast with extra bacon.

While they waited on their food, Natalie took a sip of her coffee and let out a little moan. Jackson was right—it was the best coffee. She watched in adoration as Jackson interacted with her children. He played tic-tac-toe with them on their paper placemats and talked to them about the animals on the wall. He gave them more attention than their own father, which only complicated Natalie's feelings.

All through breakfast, while they made light conversation, Jackson's knees bumped hers under the table. His eyes sparkled as bright as emeralds. Every time they touched, it was like a static shock straight to her core. Having breakfast out with Jackson and the kids seemed so normal. It felt right, like what she always thought having a family would be like. Although Natalie tried to stop him, Jackson paid for their breakfast, then walked them out.

Jackson led them down the street full of little shops. The kids' eyes got wide when they went into the candy shop, where they had everything from gumballs to chocolate-covered "bugs." Colored sodas were lined up behind the counter and bags of cotton candy hung from the ceiling. Natalie let each of the kids pick a couple of things to take with them for later.

After leaving the candy store with their treats, they walked farther down the street, glancing in shop windows. The kids laughed at funny T-shirts and admired cute animal figurines. When they got to the toy store, Emma grabbed Jackson's hand and pulled him in, like it was the most natural thing in the world to do. Emma moved around, looking at all the toys, games, and trinkets. Noah gravitated toward the books. On the way out, Jackson bought them each a stuffed animal.

A couple of hours passed before Jackson had to go back to the station. They walked toward the diner where they'd left their vehicles. In the parking lot, he told the kids he'd see them later, gave Natalie a wink, and left in his truck.

Natalie and the kids loaded their purchases into the van and drove to the grocery store. She picked up some more bread, cheese, and other staples to get them through the end of their trip, adding extras of everything in case they had more company. She grabbed some ice for the cooler and they started to make their way to the campground. It was past lunchtime, so Natalie made a quick stop back at the diner along the way and grabbed some burgers to eat at the campsite.

After lunch, Natalie took the kids down to the fishing pier. Her dad was always too busy to take her fishing, but during the summers with her grandparents, her grandfather taught her to fish. He taught her to cast, and made her bait the hook and take her fish off the line by herself. He was the reason for her love of the outdoors.

Fishing with the two kids was a challenge.

Natalie helped Emma cast out her line, and showed her how to reel it in. Only a moment passed before Emma shouted, "Mommy! Mommy! I caught one!" She reeled and reeled but her line didn't budge.

"Emma, honey, you caught a log—not a fish," Natalie told her daughter tenderly.

While Natalie tried to get her unsnagged, Emma asked the question Natalie had been waiting on for days. Even though she'd been expecting it, it still pulled at her heartstrings.

"Mommy, why didn't Daddy come camping with us?"

Natalie stopped fighting with the tangled line and knelt down by her daughter. Giving her the most honest answer she could, Natalie replied, "Daddy's very busy at work, so he didn't have time to come camping with us. Maybe he can come next time."

Noah grumbled, "Dad's always busy with work. He never has time to do anything."

Natalie didn't know how to respond because what Noah had said was one hundred percent true. The fact that the kids were noticing put yet another crack in her heart. She hated that their father couldn't be bothered to find time to be with them. While she considered what to say, Emma turned the crack into a full on fissure.

"It makes me sad that Daddy's not here."

"I know, honey. It makes me sad too." Natalie hugged Emma, willing the hug to take away her daughter's sadness. The moment was broken with Noah's shout.

"Mom! I've got one!"

"Reel, Noah!"

Noah spun his reel but when it was nearly to shore, the line broke and the fish swam away. They were not off to a great start.

For the rest of the afternoon, Natalie was back and forth between the kids, untangling lines, taking off fish, and baiting hooks. The kids had a blast, but Natalie was exhausted. Along with exhaustion came a barrage of self-doubt. One afternoon of fishing wore her out—how would she juggle life as a single mom? How would she keep up with school, sports, and friends, along with everything at home? How would she be able to give her all to the kids and not lose herself in the process? Would she be enough?

When the kids grew bored with fishing, Natalie helped them pack up their things and ushered them back toward the campsite for dinner.

With their bellies full of peanut butter and jelly sandwiches, Natalie took the kids over to the playground to get out the last of their energy. As she sat watching them swing to see who could go the highest, she realized she missed Jackson. It was ridiculous. She'd been with him all morning. She had no reason to miss him, except she hadn't seen him since he left them in town. Not even a glimpse around the campground. And while she missed Jackson after only a few hours, she didn't miss Dave after weeks.

How could she miss a practical stranger and not her husband? As she contemplated why, she thought back to their morning with Jackson and how attentive he was with the kids. She could almost feel a physical pull toward him. She thought about Noah's comment while they were fishing. She knew in an instant the answer to her question. She didn't miss Dave because he was never there to begin with. Even when he was physically around, his mind was always on work.

Natalie's heart rate picked up when she heard a golf cart approach, but settled again in disappointment when she saw it was Marge in the driver's seat.

"Evenin', Natalie." Marge took a seat next to Natalie on the wooden bench. "Your kids seem to be enjoying themselves."

"Hi, Marge. They're having a great time. I'm so glad we came here."

"And are you enjoying yourself? Perhaps with a certain tall, dark, and handsome park ranger?"

Natalie blushed. "I am. Jackson has been so nice and good with the kids. I wasn't sure how this would work out by myself, but he's been a great help."

"Yeah, he's a good guy—a hard worker, and quite smitten with you. He had such a cloudy-sky vibe about him when he got here, but now he's nothing but sunshine. I'd hate to see him get his heart broken." The look on Marge's face said this was a warning.

"I'm married, Marge. We're just friends. Jackson knows that."

"His head may know that, but I'm not sure his heart does."

Natalie didn't respond. *I'm not sure my heart knows, either.* Marge changed the subject, asking about the kids and life in the city.

They chatted for a while and when Marge stood to leave, Natalie caught her hand and gave it a squeeze. "Thank you, Marge."

"Actually, it's Alyssa."

"Alyssa?" Natalie questioned. "Then why does Jackson call you Marge?"

"It's what he knows me as. It was my nickname in college and I just got in the habit of introducing myself that way."

"Why Marge? It isn't exactly short for Alyssa."

"No, it's short for *Margarine*. I had a full rugby scholarship in college. I had a tendency of slipping through the opponents' grip, so my teammates started calling me Margarine. Eventually, it was shortened to Marge."

"Do you like being called Marge?" Natalie asked, familiar with bad nicknames that stuck.

Marge shrugged her shoulders. "Not particularly."

"Well, then, Alyssa it is. Have a good night...Alyssa."

Alyssa left to close up the ranger station and Natalie started to round up the kids. When they arrived at the campsite from the playground, there was a mason jar full of flowers on the picnic table with a note that just said *See you tomorrow. –J*

Jackson

Jackson needed to do a supply run for the campground (and he owed Marge that Starbucks), so he went into town after he had returned to his cabin and cleaned up. He decided to stop in at the diner for a quick breakfast before his errands. He'd just started looking at the menu when a burst of strawberries preceded his favorite campers walking through the door. He waved them over to join him.

As they enjoyed their breakfast together, Jackson savored every accidental touch under the table. The mate bond made him desperate for contact, and every little bit helped.

While they walked down the streets after leaving the diner, he couldn't help thinking how he could get used to this. Taking the kids to breakfast, browsing shops, spoiling them, and just spending time as a family. He wondered if it was a coincidence that both kids picked a wolf when he offered to get them a stuffed animal.

Jackson lost track of time as he got caught up in the morning. He checked his watch and discovered how late for work he was. He told Natalie and the kids that he'd see them later and then went to run his errands. Before he returned to the campground, he stopped at the jewelry store. He'd noticed Natalie admiring the charm bracelets but knew she would never buy anything for herself. Jackson picked out a few charms and had the clerk wrap up the bracelet in a nice box. While he waited, his phone buzzed and he saw a text from his brother Travis.

> Dad said you've got a bad case of blue balls. You should probably have that looked at, brother.

>> Shut up, you crude neanderthal. He did not say that.

> Oooooh. Big scary words.

> It's true, isn't it?

>> ....

> Happy for you, brother.

>> Don't get too excited. She's married.

> My big brother is a homewrecker? This just gets better and better.

>> You're an idiot.

>> And I'm not a homewrecker. Hence the blue balls.

> Go get her, tiger. 😉

Jackson rolled his eyes. His brother couldn't take anything seriously. Of all the siblings for his dad to blab to...

After grabbing the last of the supplies on the list, he bought Marge a venti dark roast, per her request, and also a latte and an iced energy drink she could stick in the fridge for later. He selected a few cake pops and baked goods and headed back to the ranger station.

"I'm so sorry, Marge," he said as he walked in, loaded down with her goodies. "I lost track of time."

"Wouldn't have anything to do with a certain camper and her kids that just returned from what looked like a very successful shopping trip, would it?"

Jackson just rolled his eyes with a smile on his face and set her treats on the counter.

"That's what I thought. Good thing you brought extras."

Jackson shook his head. "There have been some reports of a wolf in the area. Have you noticed anything?"

A funny look crossed Marge's face but quickly cleared before she answered. "No. I've never heard of any wolves in the area. It's probably a large coyote or someone's dog."

"I'm going to check some of the more popular trails for any signs of predators. We'll want to warn campers to stay on the paths just in case. Even a large coyote could be dangerous." He set out toward the nearest trails and let his senses extend for any sign of a wolf or shifter in the area. Once he'd covered all the trails, he ducked into the trees, shifted, and searched the woods.

Throughout his entire search, his thoughts were on Natalie and what a perfect morning they'd had. Of course, she never left his thoughts these days. He missed her and it had only been half a day. He wanted to see her smile and hear her laugh. Tomorrow was their last full day and he was dreading what came next.

Jackson had shifted back to human and was on the trail to the station when his phone rang. Surprised he even had service, he checked the caller ID and saw it was his sister. "Hi, Sarah."

"Hey, big brother. Dad said you met your mate? When do I get to meet my new sister?"

Jackson groaned. "Did Dad call the whole family?"

"He's excited for you. All he's ever wanted is for his golden wolf boy to find his mate."

"Sarah..." Jackson sighed. He always feared resentment from his siblings over his wolf. He never felt his wolf made him superior to his siblings. They were all amazing without it. However, he knew being the only wolf out of five could produce some jealousy.

"I'm just teasing. I was dropping the girls off with Mom for a sleepover when you called Dad. Seriously, Jackson, what's the story?"

"I met her. She's the kindest, most selfless, most beautiful human I have ever met."

"But?"

"But she's married."

"Oh, Jackson." The pity ran thick in Sarah's voice.

"She has two kids. They're beautiful, just like their mother. Noah is so smart and Emma is a spitfire. They're so much fun. But they're a family. I can't break up a family. Or a marriage." Jackson's heart hurt just talking about it.

"So what's she doing there without her husband?"

"They're separated. He walked out on Natalie and the kids and hasn't seen or spoken to them in weeks."

"Well, Jacks, it sounds like the marriage is already broken."

"What if she wants to be with him? He's the father of her children. I'm only the friendly park ranger she just met. What am I supposed to do, Sarah?"

"You fight for her, Jackson. Show her that he's not worth going back to. Dad would say, 'Fate brought her to you for a reason.' Don't give up."

"What would you do if Nate walked out and you found someone else?"

"I would do what's best for my kids, and for my heart. Even if that meant leaving their father."

"Thanks, Sarah."

"Miss you, big bro."

"Miss you too, sis. Give my nieces a kiss for me." Jackson ended the call with a lot to think about.

It was dusk when he got back to the station, feeling completely exhausted. He'd run for miles and didn't find any trace of shifter or wolf. Either it had moved on or it was very good at covering up its scent. The lack of evidence put Jackson even more on edge.

Before he made the drive to his cabin to shower and eat, Jackson stopped by Natalie's site. She wasn't there but he heard kids' laughter from over by the playground. He left her a jar of flowers he'd picked along the trails with a note saying he'd see her tomorrow. Then he went to take care of things at the cabin before he made the trek to the trees outside Natalie's tent. It had become his nightly routine to watch over her, though he couldn't say he was getting much sleep.

Chapter Nine

Natalie

Natalie got the kids cleaned up and into bed. Emma was asleep instantly. Exhausted, Natalie got ready to turn in. As she lay in bed, her thoughts went to Jackson, as they had since that first night by the fire. She was drifting off to sleep when the ever-present shadow moved into view.

Natalie was determined to settle this once and for all. She didn't like thinking she was crazy. She tiptoed around the tent, looking for her shoes and a flashlight. When she moved to the tent door, her hand paused on the zipper. *Is confronting a wolf really a good idea? Probably not. I'll just take a peek.* Worst case, she could throw her flashlight and get back in the tent. Not that the tent offered much protection from an angry wolf.

As slowly and quietly as possible, she unzipped the tent just in time to see something—or someone—move into the trees. At first, she thought she saw a large fluffy tail disappearing into the dark. She stepped just outside the door, ready to duck back in if needed, and pointed her flashlight toward the tree. The light didn't land on fur, however, but on tan muscles and dark hair that she recognized in an instant. "Jackson?"

"Natalie, I—I..." He moved into view and was completely naked.

She tried to divert her gaze from the mass in front of her. In any other situation, this would have been cop-calling territory, but with Jackson, she had to believe there was a reason for him to be naked by her tent. She couldn't bring herself to believe that the Jackson she'd gotten to know the last few days would be doing anything indecent.

Snapping her thoughts back to why she came out in the first place, Natalie looked around the woods frantically with her flashlight, looking for a glimpse of fur, or glowing eyes, any sign that a wolf was nearby.

"Jackson! You need to move. It's not safe there."

"It's okay, Natalie. It's safe."

"But...the wolf...it was just..." Natalie stammered in confusion. "I know I'm not crazy. I saw the tail. It must have walked right past you. Didn't you see it?"

"You're not crazy. You saw what you thought you saw."

Natalie's face scrunched and she rubbed her hand over her forehead. Jackson wasn't making any sense. If he knew the wolf was there, why was he just standing there—without clothes on?

Natalie's eyes jumped to Jackson's and the realization hit her. Those eyes. She had always felt there was something unnatural about them. And then there was the insane connection she'd felt from that very first night. They way she felt the same security with him as she did with the wolf. It was just like that movie Lacey made her watch, with vampires, and men turning into werewolves.

"It's you. You're the wolf." It wasn't a question. She couldn't believe what she was saying.

"I am," was all Jackson said, waiting for her reaction.

She was trying to look away, but her gaze kept moving toward his hard chiseled body. She flushed again and looked at her feet. "How?"

"I'm a wolf shifter. I've been shifting into the wolf and... keeping watch." He started to step toward her but then froze in place. He grabbed one of the towels off the line and wrapped it around his waist. He continued to move toward her. A part of her brain told her to run, but her heart told her she didn't need to be afraid. Jackson was someone important, regardless of what he was. He was now standing right in front of her. He lifted her chin with one gentle finger, looking deep into her eyes. "You're not afraid?"

She should have been terrified, but she wasn't. Not even close. With him standing this close, looking in her eyes, touching her, arousal started to grow deep in her abdomen. She looked into his eyes, looking for anything that showed he wanted to hurt her. But what she saw wasn't threatening at all. It was wanting. It was the same flame that burned within her.

"No," she spoke softly. "I am not afraid. Every rational cell in my body is screaming at me to run. But I'm not afraid at all."

Jackson

Jackson had just gotten outside Natalie's tent and settled into his wolf form when he heard the zipper. *Crap!* He started to shift and move into the trees. He wasn't sure how he was going to explain his lack of clothes if he got caught, but at the time, it seemed easier than explaining he was a wolf. However, his wolf didn't want him to leave Natalie and the shift was slow. He heard Natalie's voice question, "Jackson?" It was time to reveal his secret. *Well played, Fate.*

He waited while Natalie worked out what he was. He wanted to make sure she had all the time she needed to process. She wouldn't, however, look him in the eyes, and her face was redder than he'd ever seen it. He thought she was scared of him until he remembered he was standing in front of her buck-naked. When he moved toward her to grab a towel, he expected a flinch at the very least, but she didn't move a muscle. *That's my girl. My mate.* Now that he was standing right in front of her, staring into her eyes, her scent was intoxicating.

He needed to know for sure, needed to hear her confirm that she wasn't afraid of him. He didn't want to traumatize her. When she said she wasn't afraid, his heart exploded. He closed his eyes, leaning in closer. This was it. This was his mate. He wanted to sweep her up and kiss her senseless. Then a sharp pain hit and he remembered—he couldn't have her.

He opened his eyes and leaned back, still standing close. She hadn't retreated, but her heart was pounding and he could see the conflict in her eyes. At the same time, the smell of her arousal was ready to knock him out. Still making eye contact, she cleared her throat and squeaked out, "Umm, Jackson?"

"Yes, Natty?" The nickname came out of nowhere.

"Why are you naked?"

Jackson chuckled. "Have you ever seen a wolf in clothes?" he asked, eyebrows raised.

Natalie giggled. "No, I guess not." Jackson could see the questions swimming in her eyes, but if he stood this close to her any longer in her thin little tank top and shorts, he might do something they'd both regret.

Jackson took a step back. "It's getting late. You can ask me anything you want on our hike tomorrow—if you still want to go, that is."

"Oh, okay," Natalie responded quietly, a hint of hurt in her voice. She turned and went to unzip the tent.

Jackson started to retreat into the woods and back to his cabin. Now that she knew what he was, it might be awkward for her to have him sleeping outside her tent.

"Jackson?"

"Yes, Natty?"

"Will you be sleeping out here tonight?" Natalie asked timidly.

Maybe it wouldn't be as awkward as he thought. "I will if you want me to."

"That would be nice. I've felt safe having a wolf protector." She moved toward the tent again, turning back one more time. "And Jackson?"

"Hmm?"

"I'll see you tomorrow." With that, she disappeared into the tent.

Jackson let out an exhale. That went far better than expected. He hadn't planned for her to find out what he was, but a huge weight was lifted off his shoulders now that she knew. He still had a lot of things to explain, but she didn't scream and run away, and that was the most important thing. Not only did she not run, but she was aroused. He could feel the heat coming off from her in waves. She probably felt the same heat from him as the towel around his waist turned into a tent. This was going to end poorly.

Jackson decided then and there that he was going to fight for his mate. He was going to show her how a loving partner treats his woman. He was going to try like hell to get her to choose him, but he had to do it without crossing any lines. And he only had a day.

Jackson was getting ready to shift into his wolf and take his place when he heard a soft voice say, "Good night, Jackson."

"Good night, Natty."

Chapter Ten

Natalie

N*atty.* She hadn't heard that name in a long time. Natty is what her mother had called her. She had never told anyone. Much better than Lee, but Dave had never asked her opinion. Natalie sank down onto her air mattress. Her head was still spinning from what just happened. The sexy park ranger who had befriended herself *and* her children, the man who checked all her boxes, was a werewolf? *Not a werewolf. What did he call it? A wolf shifter.*

She didn't know why she wasn't scared. She also didn't know why she instantly believed everything he said, and didn't think he was just a creeper, naked outside her tent, doing who knows what. But she did believe him, every word. Without a doubt, she knew that Jackson was the wolf outside her tent every night. Even now, as she saw the unmistakable wolf shadow on her tent wall, Natalie knew she was safe.

Questions filled her mind and kept her awake. She tried

to keep a mental list of what to ask Jackson tomorrow on their hike. *Am I crazy for going?* He could turn into a wolf and kill her at any moment, though Natalie knew he wouldn't. When he had turned to leave, it felt like a pin pricked her heart.

Natalie realized that although she might not be afraid of Jackson being a wolf, she was afraid of her feelings for him. She twisted the ring on her finger. Jackson was making her feel things she hadn't felt from Dave in a very long time, and some things never at all. *Dave is my husband. I love him... Don't I?* She wasn't so sure anymore.

Even if she ended things with Dave, she didn't know if she could fully open herself up to Jackson. What if she misjudged him as much as she had Dave? While she didn't think that was the case, she didn't know if her thoughts could even be trusted.

Exhausted from the day's adventures and revelations, Natalie finally fell asleep.

The sun was high in the sky when Natalie woke. The kids were still sleeping and the wolf shadow was gone. As she rubbed the sleep from her eyes, she smelled something delicious outside. *Eggs and bacon?* Natalie quietly exited the tent and saw Jackson cooking over her firepit.

"Good morning, beautiful," Jackson said as he handed her a plate.

Her eyes widened as Jackson kissed Natalie's cheek. A warmth radiated through her.

"I thought you might be tired of cereal."

"Thank you. You didn't have to do this," Natalie replied sweetly. She could sense that things had changed between them after her discovery last night. Jackson seemed lighter, happier even.

"I wanted to. I have some errands to run but I'll be back

to pick you up around six." With a smile and a wink, Jackson took off into the woods.

It was a warm day, so Natalie and the kids spent the morning down at the little beach again, playing in the water. The minutes dragged on while Natalie waited for six o'clock to come.

While she lounged on her towel watching the kids, Natalie fell into a daydream. She was in Jackson's arms, pressed against that hard naked body that she had seen oh-so-much of last night. He ran his hands over her body as he held her. Up and down her back they moved, drifting lower each time. As she leaned her head up to kiss him, his face morphed into that of a wolf. At that moment, a shriek pulled her out of her reverie.

"Mommy! A fish just tickled my foot!" Emma yelled. Natalie laughed and got back in the water to play a little more, pretending to be a fish and going after their feet.

Jackson

Jackson had snuck out to his cabin to get clothes and some breakfast supplies as soon as dawn struck. Natalie and the kids were still asleep when he returned to their site and started a fire. Natalie exited the tent as he finished the eggs. Not wanting to give her a chance to change her mind about their hiking plans, Jackson handed her the plate and retreated through the woods toward his cabin. Since it was daylight, he remained in human form, keeping to the trail and whistling as he went along.

Back at his cabin, he sent out some more resumes, had an interview call, and did chores around the house. He was folding laundry when his text notification sounded. He picked it up hesitantly, not in the mood for his brother's nonsense. But the name he saw surprised him, as did the multiple messages that followed.

> Hi honey, it's Mom. I hope you're doing well. Dad said you met your mate. That's wonderful! I hope we get to meet her soon. She has kids too? I can't wait to have more grandkids to spoil.

> Anyway, everything is going well here. Dad and Isaac have been busy getting the trees ready for picking season. Doc Jones was out to preg check the goats, looks like we'll have some kids around

> Christmas. I hope to hear from you soon. LOL Mom.

Jackson chuckled. His mom had always been reluctant to use technology. He and his siblings had been trying to get her to text for years. Apparently she'd figured it out—kind of.

> Hi, Mom. Who taught you to text?

> Your sister. She said if I wanted to talk to my kids I had to text. LOL

That has Isabella written all over it.

> Can I ask you a question? When you met Dad, what was it like for you?

> Like all the magnetic force in the world was pushing me toward him. It was overwhelming, but in a good way.

> I knew right away he was special.

> And if you had been with someone else at the time? What do you think would have happened?

> Oh honey, I don't think there's anything that would have kept me from your dad.

There was something else Jackson wanted to ask, but he wasn't sure it was a conversation he wanted to have with his mom. But not knowing any other shifter mates, he didn't have another option. At least he didn't have to do it in person, or even on the phone. Somehow, texting seemed like the better choice.

> Without giving the details, what was mating like for you?

> Oh! It was very passionate. Fast but powerful. I had a very strong desire for your father to bite me. 9 months later, you were born.

> Eww, Mom.

> Grow up, Jackson. You're 34. And you asked.

> I said no details.

> Well then, it was lovely. Is that what you want to hear?

> Thanks, Mom.

> Of course, honey. IMY. CHS. LOL

> ?

> I miss you. Come home soon. Lots of love.

Jackson couldn't help but laugh. Clearly, Isa's texting lesson was not all-inclusive.

> You can't acronym everything, Mom. People won't know what you're saying. LOL means laugh out loud, but lots of love to you too.

Jackson smiled as he got a backpack ready for their hike with snacks and water, flashlights, bug spray, and emergency supplies. He hoped Natalie felt similar to what his mom felt.

When he was ready to go, he looked at the clock. It was only one. Jackson lay down on his bed and started replaying the previous night's events.

Never in a million years did Jackson think it would be easy to tell someone his secret. He imagined screaming and running. He thought he'd be pleading for her to understand. Worst case, he thought he'd be on the run if she went to the authorities. However, Natalie didn't pause even for a second. She didn't question him or call him crazy. She just accepted him, zero doubt reflected in her eyes. If only that were enough.

Just thinking about Natalie had him hard and ready.

His wolf wanted him to mate and wanted him to mate *now*. Being alone with her in the woods, surrounded by nature, with plants and animals echoing the mating call was going to take every ounce of control he had. Kissing her cheek earlier had only fueled the fire, but he couldn't resist. He couldn't give in fully, but he couldn't keep away, either. It was pure torture. *Is this really better than walking away?*

After another long, cold shower that provided little relief, Jackson puttered around the cabin until it was time to go. He took his truck this time and parked at the ranger station. He signaled to Marge that it was time and headed to site 11.

As soon as Emma saw Jackson, she went running toward him.

"Hi, little duck!" Jackson called to her as he swung her up into his arms. She babbled to him all about the turtle they saw in the river today and the fish that tickled her toes. He listened attentively, giving *oohs* and *aahs* in all the right places.

Natalie watched the entire interaction from her seat at the picnic table with a smile on her face. Jackson plopped Emma down into her chair, which made her giggle. Noah was tucked into his chair reading a comic. Jackson ruffled his hair as he walked by. Noah grinned while he playfully swatted Jackson out of his hair and went back to his comic.

Just then, Marge pulled up in the golf cart. "Hey, kids, wanna go for a ride?" Natalie stopped them before they could run to the cart.

"You be good for Alyssa. Do what she tells you and don't go running off. I'll be back before bed." She gave them each a hug and a kiss on the top of the head. The love she had for her children was almost visible, swirling around them.

"Alyssa? Her name is Marge," Jackson corrected.

"Actually it's not—right, Alyssa?" Natalie said, raising her brow in Marge's direction.

Marge, or Alyssa, grumbled, "She's right."

"Why did you tell me your name is Marge?" Jackson asked.

"Marge is a nickname I got playing college rugby and it stuck. But Natalie helped me realize that I don't have to be Marge if I don't want to. I can just be Alyssa."

Jackson looked between them, words escaping him.

As the kids rode off with Alyssa, Natalie turned, locking eyes with Jackson. She smiled a big beautiful smile, the biggest he'd seen yet.

"Shall we?" he asked, holding out his hand toward the trails. She nodded and started walking in that direction.

Chapter Eleven

Jackson

They walked in silence for a while, carefully stepping down slopes and over roots. This trail was one of the more difficult ones that most of the tourists avoided. The terrain flip-flopped between uphill and downhill, with roots and fallen trees all around for about six miles. Some man-made steps had been put in place where things got dangerously steep.

Jackson expected an onslaught of questions from Natalie, but she was eerily quiet. He hoped fear from last night hadn't caught up to her and changed her mind. He decided to break the ice. "How about a game? You can ask me whatever you want, and in return, I get to ask *you* whatever *I* want."

"Okay," Natalie replied timidly. "How did you become a wolf? Did someone bite you?"

Jackson smiled at her eagerness. "No. Shifters aren't made, they're born. We have a gene passed down through generations, although there's only a small chance that a child will become a shifter. The whole biting thing was just made up for the movies." He glanced toward her and scolded teasingly, "That was two questions—now it's my turn. What was your mom like?"

"Not starting out easy, now are you? My mom died when I was Emma's age, so I didn't know her that well. But from what I remember, she always smiled, even when she was sick. She loved to read. She would read me bedtime stories every night until she could barely speak." Natalie paused, as if she were accessing her most distant memories. "She loved music too. There was always something playing in the house. She talked about how there was a perfect song for every situation."

Jackson thought he started to see tears well up in Natalie's eyes, but she quickly blinked them away and asked her next question. "If the biting thing isn't true, is anything else from the movies?"

"Whoa there, I still have another question." Jackson chuckled.

"Oh, yeah. Oops!"

Jackson grinned. "What's your favorite flavor of ice cream?" Natalie may be using this time to learn about shifters, but Jackson was using the time to learn about Natalie.

"Mint chocolate chip," she declared without hesitation. "So like the movies, do you howl at the full moon? Or fall over dead if you use a silver spoon in your coffee?"

"No, none of that. The full moon holds no significance other than providing good lighting for a run. I can turn into my wolf whenever I want, regardless of the moon cycle. Silver won't kill me either, nor will any other material, unless it's through a fatal injury. You can use your silver spoon in my coffee anytime—you can't get rid of me that easily."

Jackson looked down at Natalie with a mischievous smile. "As for biting, we might have other uses for that, but it's not going to turn anybody into a wolf." His eyes sparkled with mystery at the uses for biting. "My turn. If you could live anywhere, where would it be?"

Natalie thought for a moment. "I've lived in the city my whole life. It would be nice to have a change of scenery. A little yellow house in the country with white trim and a big front porch. It should have a big yard for the kids to play in, maybe even room for some animals. It should be a short drive to a small town where everyone knows everyone. Someplace quiet and private. In the city, someone is always watching."

"You've thought about that a lot. That sounds like a wonderful place to live."

Natalie stopped to inspect a flower before she asked, "Were you the wolf we saw at the waterfall?"

"No. That's the confusing part. There could be another shifter in the area. I looked for any trace of a wolf or shifter and couldn't find anything. We need to be cautious. Rogue shifters can be unpredictable." Jackson thought for a moment about his next question. "What did you want to be when you grew up?"

Natalie giggled. "A ballerina. At least until I figured out I have two left feet. After that, I knew I wanted to be a mom first and foremost, but I thought I would end up following in my dad's footsteps and doing something business-related until then. Do your parents know you're a wolf?"

"Yes, as do my siblings. My dad is a wolf shifter too. He was so proud when I first shifted, even though I had to be homeschooled until I could learn to control it. We couldn't risk an uncontrolled shift in the middle of gym class. I always wished one of my brothers or sisters would shift so I had someone to play with, but none of them were so lucky."

"What do you have to control aside from turning into a wolf? Do you also have superpowers?"

"Shifters are stronger and faster than normal humans. We heal faster. We also have enhanced senses: hearing, sight, and smell, as well as a rapid metabolism. We can sense emotions if they're strong enough."

Jackson hesitated. He didn't know whether he should tell her everything or not. But if he was going to win over his mate, she should know what that would mean. "We can even distinguish the smell of our mate when we find them. Now, I think that was two questions again. Which means another two for me. How did you decide to get married?"

Natalie

"Can we go back to the ice cream question? That was easier."

Jackson stopped and took a sip of water. He looked at Natalie, waiting for an answer. She thought back to when she had said *yes* to Dave's proposal. Back when they were happy—at least, she thought they were. "I was lonely. My mom had died and my dad was gone a lot for work. I was old enough that I didn't need a nanny anymore, so I didn't even have Eloise. When I met Dave, he was charming, easy to fall for. He used his ambition to paint a pretty picture of our future. I saw it as a way to not be alone anymore. I thought he would take care of me and I wouldn't have to be a burden to my dad anymore." Natalie paused. "I thought Dave could work his way up the corporate ladder and I could be the loving wife and mother he'd come home to. And he'd be the loving husband and father coming home."

"And yet here you are, alone."

Natalie turned on him defensively. "I'm not alone. I have my kids. With them, I'll never really be alone." But the truth was, she was lonely. As much as she loved her kids, they didn't keep her warm at night. She couldn't talk to them like she could a partner. They helped ease her loneliness, but there was still a part of it that they couldn't chase away. "I always thought Dave would get settled in his career and then we could spend more time as a family. But I think I missed the part where he'll never be settled."

Natalie wasn't anticipating the next question and she was taken aback when she heard it. She could tell by Jackson's face that he hadn't meant to ask it.

"Do you love Dave?"

Natalie wasn't sure how to answer. She'd been asking herself that same question. She thought she loved Dave—that's why she married him—but she was starting to think she didn't know what love was. Where she stood now, love looked an awful lot like cooking her breakfast, playing with her kids, leaving little notes, and telling her she was beautiful even when she didn't feel it.

"I don't know," Natalie said, almost silently, but she knew Jackson heard it.

Letting the moment pass, Natalie asked her next question. "Does anyone else know you're a shifter?"

"No, and you can't tell anyone. Shifters aren't widely

known. I can't imagine the world would react kindly if they found out. While there aren't any specific rules about it, my dad always made sure we knew the secret stays in the family."

Natalie understood. She couldn't imagine telling anyone about shifters anyway. No one would believe her.

"Next question. Cats or dogs?" Jackson asked.

"Both."

"You can't have both. You have to choose." Jackson had a playful look in his eyes. She knew there was a right answer in his mind. Being a canine himself, she imagined he wasn't a fan of the felines.

"Well, if I have to choose, I'd have to say...cats." Natalie gave him a smirk and then caught a different look in his eyes. She had provoked a predator.

She began to trot away as she lightly jumped over obstacles. She giggled as she looked over her shoulder, checking the location of her pursuer. The last time Natalie looked behind her, Jackson had disappeared. She paused, checking her surroundings for where he had gone. She'd turned back toward the path when Jackson unexpectedly pounced toward her. Startled, Natalie lost her footing on an especially large tree root. He caught her in a dip before she could fall. Jackson didn't immediately set her down. His eyes held hers, trapped in that moment.

"Jackson?"

"Yes, Natty?"

"What did you mean by *mate*?"

Jackson set her on her feet and took her hand, continuing down the trail. "It's said that each shifter has one true mate. One person who accepts them as they are, no matter what. They recognize their mate by their distinct scent and the extreme magnetic pull to be with them. The bond with their mate is unbreakable and, once found, a shifter will never be with anyone else."

Natalie was silent. She thought she understood the implications of everything he said. She thought about how easy it was to accept that he was a wolf. She remembered how eager she was to spend time with him and how much she missed him when he wasn't around, despite the fact they had just met. She felt the spark with even the slightest touch. The pressure of his words crushed her under their weight. *He'll never be with another woman, and I'm married to another man.*

Chapter Twelve

Jackson

Jackson felt Natalie's shoulders slump when his words sank in. He didn't mean to put so much pressure on her, but he wanted her to know the truth. He wanted her to know how much she meant to him. He kept hold of her hand as they walked, and she didn't pull away. The sun would be setting soon and he wanted to get to the waterfall. Jackson thought Natalie understood what he'd said about mates, but he wanted to know what she felt about it. He worded his next question carefully.

"What do you feel, Natty? About me?"

Natalie took a deep breath before answering. "I feel that you're important to me. I enjoy spending time with you and my kids adore you. You've helped me remember who I am. You've brought fun back into my life. And when we touch... when we touch, it's like an electrical storm through my body." Jackson squeezed her hand. He knew that feeling.

Before Natalie could ask her next question, Jackson stopped walking. They'd reached the waterfall, the sun just starting to sink below the horizon. He dropped her hand and wrapped his arm around her waist as the sun set. He didn't care about boundaries anymore. He needed to touch her, to hold her. The colors of the sky were reflected perfectly in the pool beneath the waterfall. Jackson smiled as Natalie gasped at the sight.

As she used her phone to take some pictures of the falls, Jackson took his phone out and quietly snapped a picture of Natalie. He wanted to always remember her, right here, in this moment. He thought the game was over, but her next question came softly. "Can a shifter's mate be a human?"

"Yes. My mother is human. There aren't enough shifters, so without mating humans, our species would die out."

"Jackson...am I your mate?"

"Yes."

Natalie

Yes. That one little word rang in her ears. Everything made sense—her attraction for Jackson, her immediate trust in him, her feelings of security. She'd suspected it when he explained mates, but needed him to confirm it. She was his mate, and there was nothing she could do about it.

Dave was the father of her children and her husband of ten years. She didn't know if he'd lost himself trying to support his family or if his true colors were showing, but she thought she owed it to her kids and herself to find out. She shouldn't let ten years of marriage get thrown away based on a few days with a wolf who was telling her she was his mate.

Just that thought made her heart hurt. Thinking about not being with Jackson felt wrong.

They stood in silence as the sun continued to set. When it was almost down, Jackson gave a tug on her hand. "We need to go before it gets too dark," he said as he pulled a couple of flashlights from his bag. They made the return trek to the campground without a word passing between them.

Jackson stopped her along the river before they turned toward her site. He spun her to face him and took both her hands. "Natalie, you are my soulmate. I know that complicates things for you, and I understand. You have to do what's right for you and your kids. If I can't be the love of your life, I'll be whatever you need me to be—whatever you'll let me be. Friend. Confidant. Guard dog. If you need me to walk away...I'll try. But just know, there will never be another woman for me. You are my everything. I'll spend the rest of my days loving only you."

Natalie looked up into his eyes, not knowing what to say. *Loving me? He loves me?* He was only a breath away. If she just got on her tiptoes she could...

She glanced over his shoulder and suddenly, her jaw dropped and her heart stopped. "Jackson, I'm so sorry," was all she could get out. She dropped his hands and took off toward her campsite.

Parked next to her van was a shiny black BMW. *Dave.*

Chapter Thirteen

Natalie

Natalie's steps quickened as she moved toward her site. *What is he doing here?* As she got into view, she saw Noah and Emma in their pajamas and playing a card game with Alyssa at the picnic table. Dave paced back and forth across the site, still in his dress clothes from work. He looked up when he noticed her approaching. She could tell by the scowl on his face that he was not happy.

"Natalie! There you are! Where have you been?" Dave asked accusingly.

"Didn't Alyssa tell you? I went for a hike. What are you doing here?"

"What am I doing here? You bring our children five hours away, to the middle of nowhere, without telling me, and you ask what I'm doing here? I had to grill Lacey until she would tell me where you went. Not to mention, I got here and found that you left *my* kids with a stranger? What's going on?"

Natalie's anger started to boil over. He dared call her

out after all he'd done. "I brought *our* kids to *our* family vacation, which you agreed to. I tried to call you for weeks and you never answered. Maybe if you had, you'd have known where we were. As for leaving the kids with a stranger, Alyssa is one of the park rangers here, and my friend; she is perfectly safe."

Natalie hadn't noticed how loud they were getting or that Jackson had walked up behind her until he spoke. "Everything okay here?"

"Yes, Jackson, everything is okay," Natalie responded, trying to calm her voice. "This is my husband, Dave. Dave, this is Officer Jackson Lake, the other park ranger here."

Jealousy flared in Dave's eyes. Natalie expected to see the same in Jackson's but he remained calm, though she noticed traces of sadness and anger peeking out from behind his composed expression. It struck her as odd how well she could decipher his emotions after only a few days.

"Thank you for the hike, Jackson. I had a lovely time," Natalie said with a nod. An indication that he didn't have to stay for this. Another nod to Alyssa signaled her babysitting duties were over. "Thank you so much, Alyssa."

Alyssa gave Natalie a sympathetic look as she walked over to the golf cart and got in the passenger seat, leaving Jackson to take the wheel.

Jackson put a hand on Natalie's shoulder. "You let me know if you need anything. I've got the night shift at the station." He squeezed her shoulder and walked slowly to the cart. Natalie knew there wasn't a night shift. They closed the station at night with an emergency number posted. It was Jackson's way of telling her he wouldn't be far if she needed him.

Dave must have thought the rangers were out of earshot as he started on Natalie again. "I drove all the way here to ask you if I could come home, only to find my kids with a stranger so you could go off and screw the park ranger in the woods!"

"I didn't *screw* anybody. Jackson is a friend, as is Alyssa," Natalie retorted. "Besides, it wasn't as if you were interested in being intimate with me, or even talking to me, for that matter. I tried to call you for weeks if only to set something up for you to see your kids. I tried but you couldn't be bothered. So I brought them here for some peace and some fun, to distract them from the fact that their dad abandoned them."

Tears started streaming from Natalie's eyes, but she didn't stop. "I didn't ask for this, Dave. I didn't ask for space. I didn't ask you to leave. When I planned this vacation, it was for all of us, you included. So you don't get to blame me for trying to keep some kind of normalcy for these kids. You don't get to accuse me of cheating when I haven't done anything while you've been off doing who knows what."

"Lee, I—" Natalie put up a hand, not letting him finish. She looked wide-eyed at where Emma was now sorting game cards by herself.

"Emma, honey, where's your brother?" Natalie asked, pushing past Dave to get to the picnic table.

"He left," Emma said without turning away from her cards, not realizing the implications of her brother's disappearance.

"Did he say where he was going?" Dave questioned.

"No."

Natalie rushed to unzip the tent, only to find it empty. She called out, "Noah?" as she searched the trees, the cars, and all around the site. He was nowhere to be found. "Dave, please go check the bathroom. Emma, honey, come with Mommy. We need to find Noah."

Natalie took Emma, and Jackson's flashlight that she was still holding, and walked to the playground and along the river. There was no sign of him. She called louder and louder, panic filling her voice. Out of nowhere, Jackson pulled up in the golf cart, as if he could sense her fear. Maybe he could.

Jackson

Alyssa had gone home and Jackson was sitting on the porch of the ranger station, brooding, when he felt Natalie's panic. He didn't think he'd ever have to come face-to-face with the man who was keeping him from having his mate. The way Dave talked to her made Jackson's claws start to push their way out. He nearly lost it when Dave accused her of cheating. At the same time, his heart broke when Natalie called him a friend. He had to get away before he shifted any further.

He sat outside and left his senses open in case there was any trouble. When he felt Natalie's fear, he jumped in the cart as his own fear emerged. *That man better not have hurt her.*

When Jackson got to the site, he saw Dave by the bathrooms, but Natalie and Emma were nowhere in sight. He heard her calling for Noah down by the river. He sped down the road until he found them.

"Natalie, what's wrong?"

"Noah is missing," she cried, her voice frantic. "Dave and I were arguing and he just disappeared."

"Get in," Jackson said as he urged Natalie and Emma into the cart and drove them back to the campsite.

He took a radio out of the cart and made sure it was on and tuned in to the right channel. He handed it to Natalie and told her to stay put. "I'll go check the trails. Radio me if he comes back."

Jackson rushed toward the trailhead while keeping an eye out for any sign of the boy. Once he was alone in the woods, he did a partial shift to extend his senses even further. His nose and mouth reshaped into a snout, his ears became pointed, and his eyes took on their wolf form. He imagined he looked terrifying, but it was dark and finding Noah was more important. He caught Noah's scent along the trail Natalie had taken the kids on earlier in their trip. He turned off his flashlight, not needing it with his night vision, and ran full-speed down the path.

Sounds of the night echoed around him. Owls hooted in the trees, crickets chirped, and small splashes of water sounded from where waterfowl slept or animals went down to get a drink. Jackson listened for any noises that didn't belong, like those a child might make, or those of a large predator. He couldn't let anything happen to Noah, it would destroy Natalie. While there weren't any major predators in these woods, a mother black bear or a startled bobcat could be a threat to a child. There was also the risk of falling into the river.

Noah shouldn't have been able to go this far in that little bit of time. He must have been running hard; the kid should try out for track. Jackson still had his scent but it wasn't as strong as if he was nearby. He continued on the trail, winding behind the waterfall. When he got to the peak behind the falls, he stopped. Noah's scent didn't stay on the trail, but drifted into the woods. It was so dark that Noah probably couldn't see the trail at all. Jackson turned into the woods, following the scent.

A few yards into the woods, the scent grew stronger. It was laced with exhaustion and fear. It had now been almost two hours since Jackson had left Natalie at the campsite with Dave. Jackson withdrew out of his shift and turned his flashlight on so Noah could see it if he was close. Suddenly, another scent hit Jackson. Wolf. Not just a wolf, but a shifter.

Jackson took a few more steps and heard a snarl. He quickened his pace until he finally got to Noah, who was cowering against a tree. In front of him was a wolf that matched the description Natalie and Emma had given the day they saw it by the waterfall. It was crouched down and snarling in Jackson's direction. Noah was shaking, tears streaming down his face, but he didn't make a sound. Jackson crouched down next to Noah and said, "Hey there, champ. It's going to be okay. Just close your eyes, and whatever you do, don't open them. Don't say a word."

With Noah's eyes squeezed tight, Jackson put his hands out, trying to placate the wolf. "It's alright now. Why don't you shift and we can have a conversation, man-to-man."

The wolf continued snarling.

"Well, if you want to play the hard way..." Jackson slowly stripped off his clothes and boots and shifted into his wolf form so he could communicate telepathically with the other shifter. *"Leave the boy alone. Let me take him to his parents."*

"How do I know you won't hurt him?" the other shifter asked.

"Hurt him? You're the one snarling and scaring him half

to death," Jackson said accusingly. The other wolf stopped snarling. Jackson responded more calmly, *"My name is Jackson. His mother is my mate. She's waiting at the campground I manage."* The other wolf's eyes widened in realization and then squinted in confusion.

"I thought you said you were taking him to his parents. Are you not...?"

"It's complicated," Jackson replied, using the phrase that had become his tagline in every conversation.

Jackson told him the shortened version: *"His mother and father are separated. I only just found out she's my mate. Her husband showed up this evening and they're both at the campground currently, so I need to get him back quickly."* As an added thought, he asked, *"Why didn't you shift when I asked you to?"*

The other wolf took one more look at Noah, turned to Jackson, and said, *"I can't."* He took off running through the woods.

Jackson quickly shifted and got dressed. He would have to deal with the mysterious shifter another day. He walked over to Noah and gently placed a hand on his shoulder.

"It's okay, Noah. It's over. Let's get you back to your mom."

Noah looked at Jackson, fear still in his eyes, but nodded his head and stood. They started toward the trail that led to the campsite.

Chapter Fourteen

Natalie

It was going on four hours since Noah went missing. Natalie had been pacing frantically until Jackson had called on the radio, saying he had Noah and they were on their way, but it would be a slow walk. Dave was moving around the campsite with his phone in the air, trying to get a signal. There were no words of encouragement. No comforting touches. No apologies. Their relationship was so strained and she didn't know how they could fix it.

Natalie had put Emma to bed and was now curled up in her chair by the fire. Dave hadn't said another word to her, and she had no idea what to say to him. He had asked to come home and accused her of cheating in the same sentence. While she didn't cheat, she *was* guilty about her feelings toward Jackson. Then again, she wasn't the one that had seemingly given up on their marriage.

"You never answered. Why are you here, Dave? Did you really come all this way to ask to come home? Why didn't you call?"

Dave rubbed his neck as he sat in Jackson's chair that was still by the fire. Natalie flinched at the action but didn't say anything. "There was a dinner. For the associates and their wives. I called Lacey to work so you could get ready and she told me you weren't home. You embarrassed me, Lee. I had to lie and say you were sick. I was angry. So today, when my meetings were canceled, I decided to come find you."

"So you came all the way here because I missed a dinner?"

"I didn't think you'd take my calls, and I thought maybe if I was still living at home, you wouldn't have missed it."

"I still would have missed it because I still would have been here, with our kids. But maybe you would have missed it too. Maybe you would have been here with us."

Dave didn't respond and Natalie knew the truth. Dave never would have come. It's more likely he would have talked her into staying home. Telling her she couldn't do it alone. Making her feel like she had to stay. She decided to ask the question that had been swimming in her mind since the day she left.

"Do you love me, Dave?"

Dave looked at her like she'd grown three heads. "What kind of question is that? You're my wife."

That's not an answer, Natalie thought. But, in a way, maybe it was all the answer she needed.

"So you really didn't screw that park ranger?" Dave asked. Natalie thought he seemed almost fearful of the answer. Or maybe it was disbelief.

"No, Dave, I've never cheated on you. But..."

Before she could finish, a light flickered as it neared the site. Natalie stood and rushed out to find Jackson carrying a sleeping Noah. It's a good thing he was small for his age.

Noah woke at his mother's cry and Jackson put him on his feet. Natalie rushed to embrace him in a giant bear hug. Tears were once again streaming from both of them.

"It's okay, Noah. You're safe. Are you hurt?"

Noah shook his head and relief washed over Natalie.

"I found him a long way off the trail, behind the waterfall. He must have lost the path in the dark," Jackson told her.

"Thank you!" That was all Natalie said in return. But her eyes said so much more. They told of her fear that something had happened to her child. They flickered with happiness that Noah had returned. They burned with the hurt from her argument with Dave. Her sadness and confusion at her feelings for Jackson fell with each tear. She felt it all in that glance, and she could tell he felt it all with her.

Jackson's sadness was a reflection of her own. Natalie averted her gaze as Dave knelt beside them. However, instead of consoling his wife and child, Dave scolded Noah for running away instead. Natalie closed her eyes tight as she tried to stop the tears. When she opened them again, Jackson was gone.

Dave ushered them into the tent for the night. Natalie watched for the wolf-shaped shadow, but it never came. Her sleep was restless as Dave snored beside her, unbothered by the evening's events.

She didn't know what she was about to say before Jackson arrived with Noah. *I didn't cheat, but...I wanted to. But...we almost kissed. But...he cares about me more than you ever have. But...I'm his mate.* All of those answers were the truth, and any one of them could have ended her marriage.

Morning came early when Dave's alarm went off at six. He got up and left for the bathroom without a word. He came back in the same dress pants from yesterday and a clean shirt. He loaded his overnight bag into his car, woke Natalie, and said, "I'll see you at home," without a word of goodbye to the kids.

Natalie began packing up their things since it was check-out day. She took down the tent as the kids ate their cereal. They got everything packed in the van, somehow a tighter fit than when they arrived.

Natalie took one last look around the campground, remembering when she saw Emma on Jackson's back, growling and spitting like a wildcat. She remembered the three of them rolling on the ground laughing. She remembered kayaking and the sound of the kids' laughter when Jackson splashed them with the paddle. She remembered pancakes and shopping. She remembered that first night when she had spilled her heart out to Jackson, and he still stuck around. She remembered it all—she always would. A single tear fell to the ground.

She drove out of the campground but stopped by the ranger station when she saw her two favorite rangers out on the porch. She and the kids got out of the van and walked over. Avoiding Jackson's gaze, she thanked Alyssa for all her help and the kids each gave her a hug.

Alyssa stood to give Natalie a hug. "Be careful," she whispered in Natalie's ear. "Don't be afraid to follow your heart."

Alyssa moved inside and Natalie was forced to look at Jackson. She didn't know what she expected to find in his eyes. Anger, disgust, maybe even hatred. But when she made contact, it wasn't any of those things. Sadness, concern, and something else filled his eyes as he looked at her for what could be the last time. Love.

Emma ran up to Jackson, hanging tight to her stuffed

wolf, and leaped into his arms. "Bye, Jackson! I'll miss you!" The sweet girl wore her heart on her sleeve.

"Bye, little duck. I'll miss you too. Be good for your momma."

"I will," she sang and ran to get into the car. Noah was the next one to shyly approach Jackson.

"Thank you for finding me," Noah said.

"You're welcome, champ, but no more wandering off on your own. Your mom needs you, just as much as you need her." Noah nodded but hesitated, not knowing what else to say. Jackson pulled him into a hug and sent him on his way.

It was just Natalie and Jackson left. They stood wordlessly, not wanting to say goodbye. Natalie started: "Jackson..." but she didn't know what else to say. Instead, she lunged forward and wrapped her arms around his waist. With her head on his chest, she just let all her feelings out through her embrace. He kissed the top of her head.

"I'm sorry, Jackson. I'll never forget this week, never forget you. This trip was magical. But I have to go. I need to figure things out, away from all of this." She waved her hand around the campsite, around him. "No matter what happens, your secret is safe with me."

"Remember what I said, Natty. I'll always be there for you. Whatever you need."

Natalie couldn't respond as she turned and got in her van, not looking back. She couldn't look back. If she did, she'd never leave. She pulled out of the campground and started the return to the life she wasn't sure she wanted. As she drove down the two-lane road through the forest and toward the highway, she thought she heard the howl of a wolf.

Jackson

When Jackson left that night after returning Noah, a crack began to form in his heart. He knew an end was coming. They couldn't camp forever. However, he didn't expect it to end like this. He thought he had one more night to be close to her, but he couldn't sleep outside the tent while Dave was inside it. He stayed all night at the station, dreading the morning when she would leave.

The sun had barely risen when the black BMW zipped out of the campground. The jerk didn't even help Natalie pack up. Jackson wanted to help, but he thought giving her some space might be better. It had been an emotional night for both of them. He sat on the porch, just waiting. Alyssa joined him with her soup-bowl-sized mug of coffee.

Finally, the overloaded van pulled up and parked next to the station. The kids came running out to say their goodbyes, but Natalie looked away. Jackson wondered if she was dreading this as much as he was.

After the kids had given hugs and retreated to the car, Natalie and Jackson just stared at each other without moving. He was glad she didn't have shifter hearing to hear his pounding heart. Before he knew it, she was wrapped around his waist in a hug. He buried his nose in her hair, filling his body with her scent. He never wanted to forget the sweet mix of strawberries and coconut.

His heart shattered when she said her version of

goodbye and drove off. A part of him knew this would always be goodbye, but the reality of it hit him harder than he expected. His hand went to the small box in his pocket. The one he should have given her, but he couldn't bring himself to do it. He thought it may have been a fear of rejection. That if she'd declined his gift, she would be fully rejecting him. But truthfully, the bracelet was an anchor to her, to what he could have had. As long as he had it, he felt like she wasn't fully gone.

Jackson's wolf howled. He dodged into the woods before anyone saw him shift. He hadn't had an uncontrolled shift since he was a child, but his claws and fangs were already out. His clothes ripped as his bones snapped and reshaped. His nose and mouth turned into a muzzle and his body was covered with fur. When he finished shifting, he began to run. He ran along the woods. Ran in the direction of the road out of the campground, maintaining enough control to stay out of sight. When the last of her scent was out of reach, Jackson let out a long, forlorn howl.

Chapter Fifteen

Natalie

The drive home was much quieter than the arrival trip. Both kids were exhausted and slept most of the way. The quiet left Natalie to her thoughts.

As soon as she pulled away from the campground, she felt a tug on her heart. Something just didn't feel right about leaving. She kept telling herself that she was doing what was best for her children. That they deserved their mother and father together, regardless of what feelings she had.

But did they deserve a mother who pushed down everything that she was in order to please her husband? Did they deserve a father who put work above all else? Were two parents in an empty marriage what was best for their children? She didn't know anymore. She had shoved aside so much of herself to make sure Dave and the kids were happy, and she was failing.

Natalie had never seen her kids as free and happy as they were this past week. They'd played and laughed more than they had in years. She'd had more fun herself, too. She thought Jackson had played a big part in that, but could it have just been the camping atmosphere? By the time she got into the city, her head hurt.

The apartment was empty when they got home. Natalie found a note scribbled on the counter.

Lee,

There is a banquet tonight I would like you to attend with me. I've made a hair and nail appointment for you at 3. Lacey will be over to watch the kids. There's a new dress for you in the closet and I'll send a car to pick you up at 6.

See you tonight,
Dave

Natalie rolled her eyes. *So we're right back to this. He couldn't have told me sooner?*

Finding the new dress in the closet, Natalie scrunched her nose in disgust. Ever since he got the new job, Dave was always buying her clothes that were outside her style—and comfort. She checked her watch; it was already after two. Too bad she didn't leave any later—she could have had an excuse to miss her appointments. She turned on a movie for the kids and hopped in the shower. When she got out, Lacey had arrived.

"Hey, girl, how was your trip?" Lacey said cheerfully.

"Come over tomorrow and I'll tell you all about it. I'm late for my *appointments*," Natalie responded, rolling her eyes, the annoyance clear in her voice.

"Natalie, you need to talk to Dave about this. You don't have to go through all this if you don't want to. You were just gone for a week. How does he expect you to be ready for a banquet?"

"I know. I will, just not tonight. It's...not the right time. I have to get going. Thanks for coming, Lacey." Natalie left for the salon.

Later that evening, Natalie arrived at the banquet alone. She tugged up and down on the red dress that showed way too much at either end of her body for her liking. She felt like a hooker, not a corporate wife. A pretty young blonde waited outside the front door of the hotel ballroom. "Mrs. Evans? Dave asked me to show you in. He got pulled into a conversation with some important contacts."

Of course, he did. Natalie followed the blonde through the crowd of partygoers. When she approached Dave, he was standing with three gray-haired men in suits. The blonde grabbed his arm and whispered in his ear. Natalie thought the girl looked awfully cozy with her husband. Dave nodded and turned toward Natalie, waving her over.

"Gentlemen, this is my wife, Natalie. Alan Nichols, Theo Nardini, and Ralph Benedict are partners in the firm," Dave introduced, pointing to each of the men in turn. Natalie shook each of their hands before they returned to their conversation.

Dave pretty much ignored Natalie for the rest of the night, only addressing her if he needed to introduce her to someone important. She was standing alone at a cocktail table, swirling a glass of wine, when her phone rang. She moved to the hallway to answer it.

"Sorry to bother you, Natalie." Lacey's voice was filled with concern. "Noah had a nightmare and woke up screaming. I'm having trouble getting him to calm down."

"He had a bit of an incident last night. It must have scared him more than I realized. I'll be home as soon as I can." Natalie hung up and went to find Dave. She found him with the blonde and another woman, both laughing at whatever he'd just said as if he was the funniest man in the world.

"Sorry to interrupt, Dave, but we need to go home," Natalie said, relaying Lacey's message.

Dave turned his head and muttered to her, his annoyance clear. "Natalie, I can't leave now. Noah is nine. He can handle a bad dream."

"Dave, *please.*"

"You coddle that boy. Lacey can handle it. He'll be fine. Go check out the dessert table. I'm sure you'll find something to take your mind off Noah."

The blonde gave her a scathing side-eyed glance. Natalie turned and walked right out the front doors. She called a cab to take her home.

When Natalie got home, she went straight to Noah's room. Lacey had him using a paper bag to try and slow his breathing.

"Where's Dave?" Lacey whispered.

Natalie shook her head, mouthing *later*. "Noah, honey, tell me what happened."

"It was the wolf, Mom. I was in the woods and it was dark and I couldn't find the path. Then the wolf was in front of me. It snarled when Jackson found me."

"It was just a bad dream, honey."

"No, Mom, it was the wolf. Jackson told me to close my eyes and not open them. But I couldn't keep them closed. I opened them just for a second and Jackson was gone and there were two wolves. They looked at each other like they were talking, but they weren't making any sounds. I closed my eyes tight and then the other wolf was gone and Jackson was there, and he brought me back."

"Jackson didn't say anything about a wolf. Are you sure it wasn't just a dream?" Natalie felt bad questioning her son, but she had to be sure. From what he said, she thought the second wolf was probably Jackson.

"I'm sure, Mom."

"It's okay, buddy, I believe you. But it's over now. There aren't any wolves in the city. Why did you wander off into the woods in the dark?"

Noah looked down, playing with a loose thread on his blanket. "I didn't want to hear you and Dad fight anymore," he said quietly. "I just took off running, hoping that when I got back, everything would be okay. But I got lost."

"I'm so sorry, buddy. It's all going to be alright. I promise."

"Mom? Are we ever going to see Jackson again? I liked him."

"I don't know, buddy." *I don't know.*

Natalie sat with Noah until he fell asleep. She slid out to the living room to find that Lacey was still there, curled up on the couch, reading a psychology textbook. "Everything okay with Noah?"

"He'll be fine. Just a bad dream. He got lost in the woods last night so it's still fresh on his mind."

"I'm sorry I had to pull you away from the party. But now you can tell me all about your trip. Who's Jackson?" Lacey asked.

"Jackson?" Just saying his name made her heart flutter. "Let's open a bottle of wine. It's a long story."

Natalie grabbed a bottle and some glasses and started from the beginning. She told Lacey everything. Well, almost everything—she left out all the wolfie parts. "I don't know what to do, Lace. I've been a supportive wife to Dave for the last ten years. We made vows, 'til death do us part. But Jackson...leaving Jackson left a hole in my heart."

"Don't take this the wrong way," Lacey said. "I love you and I love the kids. Taking this job was the best decision of my life. But Dave is a jerk. Making appointments for you, telling you to go to the gym, buying you dresses that make you uncomfortable. Leaving you with two kids all on your own. Those aren't exactly the actions of a loving husband. Should you be held to your vows if he didn't mean his to begin with?"

"He wasn't always like this." Natalie put her head in her hands. *Or was he?* What he went through with his job change definitely intensified things. When she thought back, there had been red flags all along. At the time, she thought he was being romantic, but now she just saw it as controlling when he picked all their dates. He had picked her prom dress. He'd told her which wedding dress to get and planned their honeymoon without her input. Even sex was on his terms. If she tried to tell him what she liked or didn't like, he just told her to lie back and enjoy it. Were the words she said as a teenager the only thing keeping her with him?

The front door swung open, bringing Natalie back to the present. Dave charged in, fuming. "You left the most important event of my career without telling me so that you could come drink with our nanny?"

"That's my cue to leave." Lacey leaned down to give Natalie a hug. She whispered in her ear, "Follow your heart. It will always steer you right." She gathered her textbook into her messenger bag and walked out, but not without glaring at Dave.

Follow your heart. People kept telling her that. Maybe it was time she listened.

"You embarrassed me, Natalie. Again. The partners wanted to introduce you to their wives and you were nowhere in sight. Ashley looked everywhere for you. You should have been by my side."

"I was home. Taking care of our terrified son who is traumatized from being lost in the woods. And Ashley? Is that the blonde who was glued to your arm? She watched me leave."

"I told you Lacey could handle it."

"What happened to you, Dave? When did you become so uncaring? Your child was *terrified*. He's *nine*, not nineteen. He's still just a little boy. Your priorities are all backward."

"*My* priorities are backward?" Dave asked. "I don't see you complaining about the roof over your head or the food on your table. I need this job, Lee. I'm on the fast track to making partner. Then I can give you anything you want. We can hire Lacey full-time. You can do whatever you want."

"Anything I want? Do you have *any idea* what I want? What I want is to be a family. I want us to spend time with our kids together. I want to take vacations and have picnics at the park. I want them to live in a house with a backyard where they can get fresh air. I want you to play with your kids. I want you to see their joy."

Natalie had finally found her backbone. She'd found her voice and she was going to make sure Dave knew how she felt. "I don't care about hair, or nails, or fancy dresses. I don't care about any of it. I know what I want. I want our family. I want a husband that pays attention to his kids and to me. Now, you need to decide what you want...your job or your family."

Dave sputtered, trying to think of a retort, but no words

came out. He just stood up, gave Natalie one more glance, and walked out.

Natalie burst into tears. She had needed to stand up for herself for a long time, but actually doing it took more out of her than she ever imagined. She'd expected a fight—however, she thought Dave would defend himself and tell her how much he cared about his family. Hadn't he said he came to the campsite to reconcile? Now he was leaving again. All she wanted was to save her family, and instead, she watched it walk out the door.

Natalie cried herself to sleep on the couch. She awoke to a knock on the door. When she opened it, a courier handed her an envelope. Inside were divorce papers.

Chapter Sixteen

Jackson

When Natalie's van was out of sight, Jackson made it to his cabin and shifted long enough to call Alyssa and tell her that he wasn't feeling well and wouldn't be in the rest of the day. She was too smart to think his illness had to do with anything other than Natalie, but she didn't say a word about it. He'd barely gotten off the call when he was back in wolf form and taking off running. He ran straight through the night and into the next. He finally shifted back out of pure exhaustion.

Alone and naked in an unfamiliar part of the woods, Jackson collapsed. His body shook, although he didn't know if it was from all the running, the chill in the air, or something deeper. He hadn't cried since he was a child, but he found his eyes filled with moisture.

He was a good person—he helped animals and people whenever he could. He had good parents and got along with his siblings. Why was Fate so cruel as to give him a soulmate who was unavailable? What was he going to do now? He had told Natalie he could be her friend or whatever else, but he knew that wasn't true. He understood as he watched her with Dave that he loved her too much, even after just a few days, to watch her with another man. Now that she was gone, he realized he didn't even have a way to contact her.

Jackson lay there trembling and crying for a while. When his tear ducts were empty, and the shivers were most certainly from the cold, Jackson managed to shift back into a wolf and find his way to the cabin.

The next morning, he called Alyssa and apologized to her for not showing up to work, telling her that he was still sick and needed a couple more days. She grumbled something about him needing to open a Starbucks credit card and then told him to get some rest. He stayed in bed for two more days.

On the fifth day after Natalie left, Jackson's dad called. "Hi, Dad," Jackson answered in a gravelly voice.

"Are you alright, son? You don't sound well." Since shifters don't get sick, his Dad would know something was up.

"Natalie left."

"Ah," his dad said with a pause. "And you are not trapped as a wolf?"

"I was for a couple of days," Jackson said solemnly. "Now I just don't want to get out of bed. My head hurts and there's a pain in my chest that won't go away."

"I've heard of wolves never recovering after they lost a mate, remaining a wolf the rest of their lives. The fact that you're talking to me now is a testament to your strength." His dad paused. "Perhaps because your bond was not fully formed, you will recover more quickly, though maybe not ever completely. Please be careful, son."

When what his dad said sank in, it jolted his memory of what had happened the night before Natalie left.

"Remember that wolf I told you about? I met him in the woods a few nights ago when Natalie's son had gone missing. He said something about not being able to shift. Could it be that he lost his mate?"

"It's possible," his dad said thoughtfully. "After your last call, I did some asking around. It seems some wolves have been on the move. Something is drawing them to the area. None of my contacts knew why, but I did find a note in one of the history books. It mentioned wolves gathering around a leader, or alpha, when there's a threat to their kind. I'll keep asking around, but if you come across any more shifters, see what they know."

"I will, Dad. If more wolves are coming, we'll need to be careful. We don't want to draw attention to ourselves."

"Don't stay in bed too long. Fate works in mysterious ways. Life may prove to still be worth living."

Jackson said goodbye to his dad and went back to bed.

The next day, Jackson got a call from the veterinarian in his hometown. He had done his internship at that clinic and when he reached out to Doc Jones about a job, the old doc decided it was time to retire. He was interested in selling his practice to Jackson and would like to meet with him. Being a park ranger was fun for the summer, but helping animals was always his calling. Jackson agreed and set up a meeting with him for the following week.

Then, despite his strong desire to keep wallowing, Jackson pulled himself together and went to work. The campground would be closing soon and he needed to help with the preparations.

"Hey, partner," Alyssa greeted as Jackson entered the station. "Feeling better?"

"No, not really. But I need to work."

Alyssa gave him a look somewhere between pity and understanding before picking a sticky note up off the desk.

"Natalie called. She asked me to give you this."

She handed him the yellow sticky note with a phone number on it. His heart began to pound with hope. *She called.* Alyssa gave him a knowing smile as he excused himself and went on the front porch to dial the number. The prospect of hearing his mate's voice had him in a better mood than he'd been in for days.

The call rang one...two...three times, and then everything crashed down around him when he heard: *"The number you are trying to reach has been disconnected."*

Jackson threw his phone as hard as he could, then proceeded to stomp down the steps to retrieve it. He'd never forgive himself. She'd called and he wasn't there to answer because he was too busy drowning in his own self-pity. Natalie called, and now she was gone—really gone.

Jackson kept busy at work through the weekend. He cleaned the kayaks and put them away in the storage shed. He cleaned out firepits, trimmed dead branches that might fall in the snow, deep cleaned the bathrooms, and tightened all the pipes—anything he could do to both keep busy and prepare the campground for closing.

The nights were torture. As soon as he closed his eyes, Natalie's face was there. His dreams were filled with her. Always the same dream. Natalie was in his arms. He was touching her smooth skin, running his hands down her body. He held her hands as he kissed those smooth pink lips. He ran his hands over her full breasts, gently squeezing as they filled his hands. His hands kept moving downward, over her abdomen, until they reached the edge of her silk panties, at which point he awoke every night, painfully hard. It was as if his subconscious knew that going past that point would never compare to the real thing.

Monday morning came and he was up at dawn to make the four-and-a-half-hour drive to meet with Doc Jones. He returned with a packet of financials and a purchase agreement to review and sign for the small practice. He worked through the final weekend of the campground, packed up his cabin, said goodbye to Alyssa, and arranged for his apartment in the city to be packed and moved to his new home.

Chapter Seventeen

Natalie

> Hey, girl, it's Natalie. This is my new phone number. New address to come.

What?!?! What happened?

> Dave served me with divorce papers. I'm not fighting it. Honestly, I think he just beat me to it. After the camping trip, it was only a matter of time. I'm getting out of this city.

You go, girl. I mean, I'm sorry. I don't really know how to respond in this situation. 😊

> 😊 You're a psychology graduate student. Shouldn't you be full of sage advice?

You're right, let me consult my textbooks. Please lie back on my couch and tell me how you're feeling.

> Hurt, sad, and full of regrets.

> Aww, I'm sorry, Nat. 😢 I'm here for you, whatever you need. I love you, girl.

> Love you too. 🖤

Three weeks later, Natalie waited outside the mediator's office. The days since receiving the divorce papers had been a whirlwind. With only a month left on the apartment lease, Natalie needed to find somewhere to live and hoped that her child support money would be enough while she looked for a job.

Luckily, she found a small two-bedroom house for rent in a rural town thirty minutes north of the city. The little old landlady was very kind and gave Natalie a discounted rate until she could find work. She got the kids enrolled at their new school in record time and even signed them up for soccer.

Lacey had been a big help with the move and with life as a single mom. Natalie couldn't afford to pay her as a nanny anymore, but she still helped out as Natalie's friend. Lacey had helped with school pickups and took care of the kids while Natalie pounded the pavement looking for work. They would spend evenings talking and watching chick flicks after the kids were in bed, and Lacey would often crash on Natalie's couch.

Friday, while the kids were in school, Natalie and Dave were scheduled to finalize their divorce. She hadn't tried to fight it. The fact that Dave had the papers drawn up before the banquet, before the camping trip, told her all she needed to know. He had no interest in fixing what they had. Her heart wasn't interested in a fix, either. It only beat for a certain wolf that she didn't expect to ever see again.

Dave arrived and sat next to her on the bench in the hallway of the courthouse, waiting for the mediator. They sat in silence until Dave said, "Natalie, I'm sorry it had to come to this. You just don't fit in my world anymore."

"I don't fit in your world? Your world has become so small, no one can fit in it but you," Natalie retorted. "Were you ever happy, Dave?"

"I think I was. A long time ago." The silence resumed until the door opened to welcome them in. They made it through the proceedings with very little argument. Natalie would have primary custody of the kids while Dave would have them every other weekend. He didn't think it would be possible to have them any more than that with his work schedule. Without many assets to divide, their vehicles each in their individual names, Dave agreed to the child support amount and they parted ways.

The next day, Natalie and Lacey took the kids to a nearby orchard to go apple picking. The orchard had hayrides, doughnuts, cider, and even a petting farm. The place was swarming with life. Kids were laughing and playing everywhere while their parents watched and sipped their cider. Young couples walked hand in hand through the fruit-laden trees. The sweet smell of apples filled the air.

Out in the orchard, Lacey and the kids picked some apples. Natalie, however, found herself looking at a mostly green fruit that wasn't quite ripe. She didn't know why, but the apple made her think of Jackson.

Natalie hadn't spoken to Jackson since the day they left the campground. She went to give him a call a few days after the banquet and realized they'd never even exchanged phone numbers. She tried calling the campground, but

Alyssa said he wasn't in and she didn't know when he would return. Their rules didn't allow her to give out his personal number, but Alyssa said she would let him know Natalie called. He never called her back. *So much for him always being there.*

After that day, she didn't have much time to think about him as she got her new life together. Now here, staring at this apple, her heart began to ache. She had let something so wonderful go to try and fix something that wasn't meant to be fixed. A tear made a trail down her cheek. She stood there, thinking about what could have been, until she heard a voice.

"That one is not quite ready, my dear." She turned to see a middle-aged gentleman in jeans and a plaid work shirt. He wore a big straw hat to keep the sun off his tanned neck and face. A large bag for picking apples was slung over his shoulder.

"I—I'm sorry. I was just..."

"Lost in thought?" the man finished for her. Natalie nodded. "You know, sometimes when we find something that feels right, we aren't ready for it. However, if it is truly meant for us, we will find it again when the time is right." With that, the man continued up the rows of apples.

That was so strange. Natalie hustled to catch up to Lacey and the kids. When they returned home at the end of their fun day, Natalie sent the kids to get cleaned up for bed while she checked her phone, which she'd forgotten at home. She called her voicemail and heard a woman's voice requesting an interview with her on Monday morning for an office manager position at the local veterinary office.

Jackson

Jackson kept pretty busy during the first week of his new life. He signed the papers to his new practice and got the rundown of the place from the current vet and his staff. He rented a room at the local B&B while he met with a realtor to start looking for a house. His parents offered him a room but he hadn't lived with them since he moved to the city, and he wanted his own space. In what little free time he had, he worked on getting reacquainted with the close-knit little town and finding safe places to run.

Jackson spent hours with his realtor looking at just about every house for sale in a twenty-mile radius. Most of them were fine for what he needed but didn't match the vision he had when he closed his eyes. They were down to the last one she had available, and he was ready to just pick the most efficient option and be done. However, when he saw this last house, he found himself making an offer before the tour was even finished. This new life was turning out just as he had always imagined. He was missing only one thing: his family.

He didn't know what it was about being in this town, but the scent of strawberries and coconut lingered in the air everywhere he went. The grocery store, the bakery, the coffee shop, and even the bank. Sometimes he caught it on the breeze as he walked the streets in town. Not only was he tortured by his broken heart and his chronic headache, but now he was losing his mind.

One Friday afternoon, Jackson was finishing up some work at the clinic. Doc Jones had started the process of hiring a new office manager and had reviewed resumes, but Jackson hadn't yet gotten around to calling on them. Without so much as glancing at them, he gave the receptionist the stack of applications that his predecessor had selected for interviews and asked her to make the calls the next morning. He left the office dreading a weekend without work to distract him.

On Saturday, Jackson closed on his new home and checked out of the B&B. The house had been vacant for a while and the sellers wanted it gone quickly. Not caring to shop for furniture, Jackson paid extra to have the realtor leave the staging pieces. He'd have his sisters decorate for him later. If he did it himself, they'd just redo it anyway.

One of the best parts of the relocation to this small town was the proximity to Jackson's parents. On Sunday afternoon, he made the twenty-minute drive out to the orchard. The orchard was full of life this time of year, as apple-picking season was at its peak. He drove down the private dirt drive toward his parents' house. Rows of fruit trees separated him from the public part of the farm. He had his windows down to smell the sweet apples that told him he was home, but another scent caught his attention. A very faint wisp of strawberries and coconut. *I really am losing it.*

Jackson's mom, Marie, had invited the whole family over for Sunday dinner. It had been a long time since they'd all been together. The table was full of salad, lasagna, garlic bread, and, of course, apple pie.

Jackson was the oldest of the five siblings. His oldest sister Sarah arrived with her husband Nate and their two little girls, Amber and Rosalie. Next was his brother Travis and his fiance Leah. Finally, the twins, Isaac and Isabella, came in together. They were both single college students and best friends.

Jackson quietly sat through dinner while trying to pay attention as his family discussed new jobs, wedding plans, and thesis topics. However, the emptiness he felt sitting at the table without his mate by his side was overwhelming. He watched Amber feed bread to the dog under the table and thought of all the trouble she and Emma could get into. He thought about Natalie going shopping with his sisters and the things they would find. He wondered if his brothers would give her the same hard time as they did the other girls. He imagined taking Noah out to do farm chores to teach him what it meant to work hard.

At this table, surrounded by his family, he had never felt so alone.

Jackson excused himself from the table and took his mostly-full plate to the kitchen. He found a bottle of his dad's gin and poured a glass. His shifter metabolism kept him from getting drunk, but he liked to think a strong enough drink would at least take the edge off. He had downed it and was pouring a second when his dad came into the kitchen.

"Do you want to talk about it?" Edwin asked as he found his own glass.

"It's been over a month since she left, and yet...and yet I smell her everywhere I go. I even thought I smelled her here at the orchard. I've tried to keep busy with the new clinic, but when I'm not busy, all I think of is her. Not just her, either—Noah and Emma too. I think about us as a family. I miss them all so much."

"Have you talked to her since she left?"

"I've tried. We didn't exchange numbers. She left a message at the campground while I was unwell, but when I tried to call back, the phone number had been disconnected."

Jackson downed another glass before turning to his dad. His voice turned almost pleading. "What if I never see her again? Am I going to have to live with her scent haunting me for the rest of my life? When I walked into the clinic the first time, I opened the door and her scent filled the air, as if she'd just been there. How am I supposed to move on?"

"Perhaps it's not time to move on. Keep dreaming those dreams and don't lose hope. You've still got time. You may find your mate again someday, when the time is right."

"Always the optimist, Dad." Jackson checked the time. "I have to go. I need to prepare for some interviews tomorrow morning."

"Don't forget to say goodbye to your mother. It's good to have you home, son."

Chapter Eighteen

Natalie

Monday morning came and Natalie got the kids off to school before returning home to get ready for her interview. She wore a gray pencil skirt with a turquoise blouse that brought out her blue eyes. She'd used a flat iron on her hair instead of wearing her usual frizzy curls.

After applying minimal makeup, she still had time to spare. She checked her phone, as she had a few dozen times a day since leaving a message for Jackson. Still no call. Part of her thought that he clearly didn't want to talk to her, but the other part—the part that still held hope—decided to try one more time.

She dialed the number for the campground and tried to mask her disappointment when a woman's voice answered.

"Hi, Alyssa."

"Natalie? What can I do for ya?"

"Well...umm...I was wondering if Jackson was there?"

"Oh, no. I'm sorry, hon. He left when the campground

closed. I'm just here finishing up some end-of-the-year paperwork before I settle in for the winter."

"Oh," was all Natalie could answer. Every ounce of hope left her like someone let go of a balloon.

"He tried to call, you know, after he got your message. The number was disconnected."

"Oh my gosh! Alyssa! I can't believe I forgot that I changed my number!"

"Well, that would explain it."

"I think I messed up," Natalie admitted. "I shouldn't have left like that. Was Jackson upset?"

"He was...not in a good place," Alyssa answered quietly.

"Have you talked to him? Do you know where he went?"

"All I know is he went back home to be near his parents. I think he was taking over the local vet clinic or something."

Natalie racked her brain, trying to remember where Jackson said his parents lived—if he'd mentioned it at all. "Thanks, Alyssa. Can I give you my new number in case you talk to him?"

"Sure, hon. I'll try to get it to him."

"Thanks, Alyssa. And you can use it too, anytime."

"Good luck, Natalie. If you two are meant to be, you'll find each other again," Alyssa said before ending the call.

Now that it was time to go, Natalie checked the mirror one more time before she headed off to the vet's office.

Natalie didn't hold much hope for getting the job. She hadn't worked in almost ten years, and before that, she only had one year of experience as an office assistant for a small realtor. With only a high school diploma, the options were limited, but she'd applied for everything she came across in hopes that someone would be desperate enough to give her a chance.

Natalie sat nervously in the waiting room. She'd heard the clinic was run by an older man who needed some help with things like using technology. The receptionist was part-time and mostly answered the phone and checked in patients.

Natalie was studying a poster of the different types of ticks when the receptionist said, "Natalie Brooks? The doctor will see you now."

Jackson

Jackson had sat through two interviews already, and neither was very promising. He looked at the name on the next resume and closed the folder without reading anything else. *Natalie Brooks*. There was only one Natalie he could be around: Natalie Evans. It wasn't fair to this girl, but he already knew what his answer would be.

If he'd looked at the resume, he might have seen that Natalie was a newly single mom with very little work experience, whose last job was at a real estate office in the city almost ten years ago.

He opened his desk drawer and took out the box with the charm bracelet he'd bought over the summer. He had wanted to give it to Natalie before she left, but Dave's arrival changed everything. Now it was just a daily reminder of all he'd lost.

He heard his receptionist, Cheryl, call her back. He returned the box and closed the drawer.

"Right this way, Ms. Brooks."

His office door opened and he was hit right in the chest with the aroma that had been haunting him for weeks. He didn't want this poor girl to see the look of disappointment in his eyes because she couldn't possibly be *his* Natalie. He pretended to look at her resume.

"Dr. Lake, this is Natalie Brooks," Cheryl said before returning to the front. And then he heard it. The same sweet voice that called out his name in his very vivid dreams.

"Jackson?"

Jackson slowly looked up. Before him stood a beautiful woman with long, straight, strawberry-blonde hair and vibrant blue eyes. She was dressed in a skirt and blouse that hugged every one of her curves perfectly. It wasn't the messy-bunned, comfy-clothes-wearing woman from the campground, but it was *her*. His mate.

Jackson got to his feet but his knees felt like they would buckle, so he leaned on the desk for support. "Natty?"

She nodded her head while her mouth gaped open and her eyes widened. She was completely stunned.

"It's really you." Feeling a little more stable, Jackson took a step toward Natalie.

Natalie still didn't move.

He took another step, his brows furrowed and his hands clenched at his sides as if to keep from reaching for her. "I thought your last name was Evans."

"Brooks is my maiden name."

Jackson froze. *Maiden name?*

"So, you're...?" He couldn't finish his sentence as he

took another step. She hadn't moved from just inside the door.

"Divorced," Natalie finished for him as she nodded and held up her naked left hand.

"How long?" Another step. He was standing so close now that he could hear the quickened pace of her heart beating.

"He served me papers the day after we got home from camping. We finalized it last Friday." Another step. He was right in front of her.

Jackson was barely holding it together. He had been dreading this day and now he was here, with the love of his life in his office, in his hometown. She was here and he couldn't wrap his head around it.

"I'm sorry, Natty. You called and I wasn't there. I promised I'd always be there. I called back but it was too late."

"It was my fault. I changed my number and gave Alyssa the wrong one. And I'm sorry, Jackson. I'm sorry I left like that. I'm sorry I didn't tell you how I felt. I'm sorry for everything."

Tears started to fall down Natalie's cheeks. Jackson wiped them away before he put his hands on her hips, pulling her closer, and dipped his head so his forehead was against hers. "It doesn't matter. You're here now. No more tears."

They just stood there for a moment. No words passed between them. Jackson reveled in the feeling of his mate in his hands. He could feel her pulse quicken. Her heart pounded, much like his own.

"Jackson," Natalie whispered as her palms met his chest. Her voice was pleading. He knew exactly what she needed. It was what he needed, too.

He pressed his lips to hers, and suddenly, everything they'd been feeling the last month was poured into a kiss. With the slightest touch of his tongue to her upper lip, she opened for him. Their tongues danced as their hands wandered. One of her hands tugged in his hair as the other splayed across his chest. His hands moved up to her waist and then down to her thighs. He played with the hem of her skirt with one hand while the other drew little circles on her thigh. Her hand moved from his chest, grasping his fingers and pulling her skirt even higher.

They continued their kiss with sweet abandon for several minutes. Jackson forgot why Natalie was there in the first place—he was just elated she was there at all. There and available. No, not available...*his*.

Natalie put her hands on his chest and pulled her head back to look into his eyes. They were both panting and out of breath. "Jackson...We should take it easy."

Jackson remembered they were in his office with his receptionist down the hall. He straightened her skirt, but he wasn't ready to let her go. He wrapped his arms around her. "You're right. I just...I never thought I'd see you again."

"I know, Jackson. I know." They stood there for a moment, just holding each other.

"What are you doing here, Natty? Where are the kids?"

"The kids are in school. After Dave left, the lease was up on our apartment, so I took the opportunity to get out of the city and we moved here. He gets them every other weekend so we couldn't move too far, but I couldn't stay in the city. I found a little house to rent but I need to find a job to pay for it. I applied pretty much everywhere in town."

Realization hit as she spoke. "I smelled you *everywhere*. The bank, the grocery store, here at the clinic. I thought I was going crazy."

He'd been in the same town as his mate for *weeks* and hadn't known. He thought of all the times he smelled her and the places he must have just missed running into her. He even thought about the orchard and decided he'd ask her about that later.

"When did you get here, Jackson? I thought this clinic was owned by Doc Jones. That's what I was told when I applied, anyway."

"Doc Jones called me up a few weeks ago and offered to sell me the clinic so he could retire. I came to see the place and thought I could come here to...move on."

"And did you...move on?" Natalie asked with a worried look on her pretty face.

Jackson stroked her cheek. "No, Natty. I meant what I said. You're the only girl for me." He leaned in for another kiss. This one was softer and gentler. Her little arms squeezed tight as she kissed him until a knock on the door interrupted them.

"Doctor Lake? Your next interview is here. Should I reschedule?"

"No, Cheryl," Jackson answered, almost breathlessly. "I'll be right out."

Jackson leaned his forehead against Natalie's, giving her nose a little rub with his own. "Can I see you tonight?" he asked softly.

"I have to get the kids from school at three. Why don't you come over for dinner? They'd love to see you."

He gave her one more quick kiss before saying, "I'll be there." He opened the door and she walked to the front lobby.

Jackson sat down at his desk, leaning back in his chair in disbelief. He needed a moment before his next interview, though it was just a formality. He'd already made his choice.

He couldn't believe Natalie was here. After all this time thinking he was going crazy, it was *her* he was smelling everywhere.

The most important thing was that she was here, with nothing in the way. When his heart rate had slowed, Jackson ran his hands through his hair, straightened his clothes, and gave Cheryl a call to bring back the next candidate. Before she arrived, he opened his drawer again and put the little box in his pocket.

Chapter Nineteen

Natalie

Natalie straightened herself out the best she could and walked out of Jackson's office with a smile plastered on her face. The receptionist, Cheryl, looked up at her with a slight smile as her cheeks flushed and she told Natalie to have a nice day. Natalie leaned her head against her car door. *Well, I blew that interview.*

Jackson was here.

She thought she'd missed her chance and that it would be just her and the kids for the rest of her life. For much like what Jackson had said, she had confirmed there was no other guy for her.

Natalie got in the car and looked in the visor mirror. *Oh my God.* Her hair was a mess, her lips were swollen, and her face was red with whisker burns. No wonder the receptionist blushed. What would she think of Natalie? Jackson would have some explaining to do.

Natalie stopped at home and changed into some black yoga pants and a plain turquoise T-shirt before going to get groceries for dinner. She picked up the kids on her way home. When she pulled into the driveway, there was a green pickup truck with a tall, handsome veterinarian leaning against it. Natalie had barely put the van in park before Emma was out of the car running and yelling, "Jackson!"

"There's my little duck! I missed you," Jackson said as he spun her up into his arms. Noah tried to hide his excitement, but he left his door open as he half-skipped, half-jogged over and gave Jackson a fist bump.

"Hey there, champ. Have you been taking care of your mom?" Jackson put Emma down and walked over to where Natalie leaned against the car.

Natalie put her arms around his neck like it was the most natural thing in the world. He gave her a peck on the cheek and said, "I couldn't wait for dinner."

"Good," Natalie replied with a grin. "You can help with the groceries."

"It would be my pleasure."

While Natalie got dinner started, Jackson took the kids outside to play their favorite game: wolves and deer. This time, Jackson was the deer and the kids chased him round and round until he collapsed and the two kids piled on top of him. Natalie watched out the kitchen window. This was everything she had dreamed of for her kids.

They ate dinner together, catching up on all that had happened in the last month. Jackson helped Noah with his homework while Natalie gave Emma her bath. When the kids were all tucked in, Jackson recited his favorite childhood story, *The Wolf Prince,* complete with voices and all. Natalie couldn't stop smiling while she started on the kitchen cleanup.

She was at the sink doing dishes when two strong arms

wrapped around her. "Today was perfect," he whispered in her ear.

She turned to face him, placing one hand on his chest, the other putting bubbles on his nose. She giggled as he tried to blow them off. "Yes, it was," Natalie agreed as she wiped off the bubbles. He pulled her up into another kiss.

Natalie suddenly had the sensation that she was falling as two large hands squeezed either side of her rear end and lifted her off the floor. "Jackson!" she squealed as she was transported over to the couch.

"You had a busy day. I thought you might like to get off your feet." Jackson grinned as he plopped her down on the couch. He sat down next to her, put her feet in his lap, and started rubbing them.

Natalie let out a small moan. She couldn't help herself. The only foot rubs she ever had were during a pedicure, and that just wasn't the same. She leaned back into the throw pillows. "Your hands are magic," she moaned again as he worked from one foot to the other.

"You haven't seen anything yet."

She lifted her head to see the desire burning in his glowing green eyes. She felt it too, in him and in herself. Suddenly, that scared her.

"Umm, Jackson?"

"Yes, Natty?"

"Can we maybe take it a little slow?" There it was. The disappointment overtook the desire and his eyes stopped glowing. "I'm really happy that you're here. Extremely happy. It's just…I've technically only been divorced for three days. I need to be careful. Especially with the kids."

Jackson pulled her up so she was sitting sideways in his lap. She couldn't help but notice the bulge that was now pressing against her thigh. As he swept back her hair and tucked it behind her ear, he lifted her chin so she was looking into his eyes.

"Natty, as long as I have you, we can take things at whatever speed you want."

Jackson

Jackson couldn't hide his disappointment when Natalie asked to take it slow, but he understood. While he had done nothing but dream of these moments with her for the last month, she had completely uprooted not only her life but also her children's. They had to completely start over and, just as they started to settle in, he showed up. His wolf growled at him when he promised to go at her speed. It wanted his mate claimed now.

When Natalie leaned in to give him one of her sweet strawberry kisses, Jackson held back. He was already aroused. There was no way she didn't feel it. He didn't want to lose control. But it was Natalie who teased his lips open with that delicious little tongue of hers. He let her control the kiss at first, but it seemed her body was not in agreement about going slow. The smell of her arousal was intoxicating, as were the sparks with every touch.

Jackson lowered her down to the couch. He leaned down over her, kissing behind her ear and down her neck. "Just tell me when you want me to stop," he whispered. He used one hand to hold his weight over her while the other worked its way under her T-shirt so his thumb could rub circles on her ribs.

Moving to her lips, Jackson deepened the kiss, letting their tongues tangle together like vines that couldn't be separated. He moved his free hand up to caress her peaked nipples under her bra. Natalie let out a gasp as he pinched and then massaged each nipple through the soft fabric. His little mate was so responsive to every touch. He cupped each of her breasts in his large hand before moving his hand down to her hips. All the while, their lips never separated.

As they came up for air, Jackson took the opportunity to check in. "Doing okay, beautiful?"

"More than okay," Natalie said with a sweet smile. Jackson sat up and pulled her so she straddled his lap. He buried his face into her neck, inhaling her scent and planting kisses over every part of her skin. One hand gently tugged at her hair and the other reached between her now-separated legs to rub the juncture of her thighs. The more he rubbed, the stronger the smell of her arousal became. He didn't want to push her too far, but he could sense the need for pleasure thrumming through her body.

Natalie whimpered at the absence when he moved his hand up to tease her waistband. She hadn't said much of anything, but Jackson couldn't get enough of the cute little noises she made. While he worked his hand under her waistband and down her front, Natalie began to grind against his erection as she searched for the friction she needed. When he got to the edge of her panties, a shiver spread throughout her body. Her head dropped and her eyes closed. She still didn't tell him to stop as he slipped a hand into the front of her panties.

Jackson moved his other hand from her hair to grip her ass as she continued to grind against him.

"You want this, Natty?"

"Yes! Please, Jackson," Natalie pleaded.

Oh, God, I'm not going to make it. Jackson was on the edge and could feel the pressure pushing him toward release. He ran his fingers up and down her folds, working closer to the center. She was so wet under his fingers that he could tell she needed this as much as he did.

At last, Jackson found the knot in her center. He had barely applied pressure when Natalie cried out and tremors rolled through her body. As she bucked and shook against him, his own climax came. He hugged Natalie tight to his chest as they both soaked through their pants in their release.

Natalie collapsed into the pillows panting. So much for going slow. Jackson sat up and bowed his head in his hands. His first night with his mate and he'd royally screwed it all up by dry humping her like a teenager. "I'm so sorry, Natalie. I'm so, so sorry. I should have had more control."

Chapter Twenty

Natalie

Natalie was coming down from the best orgasm of her life when she heard Jackson's distressed voice apologizing. She leaned up on her elbows and saw him with his head in his hands, rocking back and forth. She could feel panic radiating from him but she didn't understand at first what was wrong. They didn't even take any clothes off. His touch had been magical and while she was glad they didn't go all the way, she'd needed that release. She suspected he needed it even more.

She pulled herself up the rest of the way to sit next to him. Natalie pulled his hands away, threading her fingers through his, and he looked at her with guilt-ridden eyes.

"Jackson, *stop*. You didn't do anything wrong. That was incredible."

"But you wanted to go slow and I blew it." *Literally.* The look in his eyes was full of disappointment and fear. Natalie couldn't believe how sensitive he was to her wants and needs. It had never been about her before.

Natalie grabbed his face in her own hands. "You told me to tell you when to stop and I didn't. I didn't want you to." A sly smile spread across her face. "In fact, I'm pretty sure I begged for it." She pressed a chaste kiss to his lips.

"You aren't mad at me?"

"Mad? Not even a little. That was amazing," Natalie said with another smile. Jackson was on her lips so fast with a not-so-chaste kiss. Natalie's heart was so full after just one afternoon. But then, all too quickly, Jackson pulled away.

"It's getting late, I should…"

"Stay," Natalie cut him off. The thought of him leaving, even just for the night, made her heart hurt all over again. Now that she'd found him again, she didn't think she could ever be apart from him.

"Are you sure, Natty?"

"Yes, Jackson. I've never been more sure. Please stay with me."

Jackson got to his feet, nodding. "Of course," he said, and headed for the door.

"Where are you going? I meant stay with me inside, not outside as a wolf."

Jackson chuckled but continued to walk outside. Natalie, baffled, followed him to the door. She started to worry that he wasn't going to stay until he reached into the bed of his truck and pulled out an overnight bag. She blocked the door as he turned and walked toward the house.

When he got up the steps, she looked up at him. "That's a little presumptuous, don't you think?" she asked with a smile.

"Just hopeful." Jackson kissed the tip of her nose and she let him in.

Jackson

Jackson was thrilled Natalie asked him to stay—otherwise, he *would* have been outside as a wolf. No way was he leaving her now that he'd found her again.

Natalie showed him to the ensuite and he cleaned up in the bathroom while she checked on the kids. He changed into the T-shirt and athletic shorts he'd brought to sleep in, not wanting to be presumptuous, like Natalie had said. Before putting his dirty clothes in his bag, he emptied that little box and put the contents in his pocket.

What happened in the living room was unplanned, but not unwanted. However, he needed to have better control. If they'd managed to get any clothes off before their combined orgasms, he would have claimed her then and there without her even knowing what that meant. The fact that Natalie hadn't been upset with him made him feel a little better, but he'd have to be more careful until she was ready. She was too important to chase away with his eagerness.

Jackson looked at all the pictures on the dresser and bookshelf in Natalie's room while she was getting ready for bed. The kids' school and baby pictures were joined by a few from their trip. Pictures of the kids swimming, of them by the waterfalls, and selfies from around the campground had already been framed and scattered around. On her nightstand stood the picture Natalie had taken of the falls on their hike. She'd caught the sunset perfectly. Just barely visible in the water was a reflection of the two of them. It was the only picture she'd taken of them together.

When Natalie came out in her satin sleep tank and shorts, Jackson pulled her to him where he sat on the edge of the bed. He couldn't believe that this morning he woke up dreading a day of interviews and now he was going to bed with his mate. He grabbed her wrist and slipped on the charm bracelet he'd bought her.

"Jackson! What is this?" Natalie asked as she examined the bracelet.

"I bought it for you that day we went shopping in town. I knew you would never get something for yourself. I wanted you to have something to remember your trip, but I never found the right time to give it to you." He pulled her down to his lap and peppered her with kisses over her lips, cheeks, and neck. When he returned to her lips, she immediately opened to let him in. Their kiss deepened as he laid her back on the bed. Her hands roamed his arms and back. When they reached his waistband, he pulled away.

"Natty, we have to stop or I'm going to mark you tonight."

Natalie looked up at him, her features tightening with confusion. "Mark me?"

Jackson thought back to the conversation his dad had with him as a teenager. *The Birds and the Bees: Wolf Edition.*

"Shifters will...bite their mate, usually on their neck, to mark them so all other shifters know they're off limits. I didn't tell you before because I honestly didn't think it would ever happen."

Natalie's hand jumped to her neck. "You're going to bite me?" A tinge of panic filled her eyes.

"Not tonight, beautiful—not until you're ready. Once I mark you, there's no turning back, so I want you to be sure." Jackson placed his palm on her cheek. "Mating for shifters is like marriage, but more. It's not legally binding, but it's everything else. Physically, spiritually, emotionally bound together forever."

"Will it hurt?"

"I honestly don't know, but if I had to guess, it will probably hurt a little. From what I've heard, though, the pleasure it brings is well worth the pain."

The look in her eyes started to change from panic to arousal. Before things could go where Natalie wasn't ready for them to go, Jackson turned to his side and pulled her back against him. "You got the job, by the way," he said as he wrapped his arms around her. She turned toward him the best she could under his hold.

"What? No, Jackson, you can't do that. You didn't even ask me any questions."

"I thought I was never going to see you again. Now that I've found you, I want to spend as much time with you as possible. That's all I need to know. Besides, I need someone who can deal with the cats," he said with a wink. Natalie giggled. "You can start whenever you're ready."

"Jackson..." His name sounded so sweet on her lips. He gave her one last kiss goodnight and pulled her in tight.

"Good night, Natty."

"Good night, Jackson."

They both drifted off to sleep.

Chapter Twenty-One

Natalie

Natalie awoke after the best night's sleep she'd had since the camping trip. Behind her was a wall of muscle, with strong arms wrapped around her. And in front of her was a little ball of warmth. Natalie opened her eyes and saw two blue ones staring back at her.

"Mommy, why is Jackson in your bed?" Emma had snuck in sometime in the night and climbed into bed with them. Natalie would have to remember to lock the door from now on.

"What would you think if I said Jackson was Mommy's boyfriend? Would you be okay with that?" *Boyfriend* sounded inadequate, but she couldn't really say *mate* to her five-year-old daughter. It wouldn't make a difference with her, anyway. *Boyfriend* was as good of a word as anything. Natalie wasn't even sure that Emma fully understood the situation with her father.

"Will he take us for party pancakes again?" Emma asked brightly. *Of course, it would come down to pancakes.*

Jackson kissed Natalie's shoulder as he leaned up over her. "Anytime your mom says it's okay, little duck."

"Then I would be okay with it," Emma said gleefully as she skittered out of the room. Natalie turned and wrapped her arms around Jackson until, a minute later, there was a knock at the door. Noah stood in the doorway.

"Come on in, buddy," Natalie said as she rolled over and sat up on the bed. It was officially morning.

"Mom, Emma said...O*h*." He stopped when he saw Jackson sitting up on the other side of the bed. "So you and Jackson are really boyfriend and girlfriend?"

"We'd like to be, if you're okay with that." Natalie guessed it would take more than pancakes to convince Noah.

"Are you going to get married?"

"Maybe someday," Natalie said and she felt her heart pulse in excitement at the thought of marrying Jackson. "It's a little too soon for that now, though."

Noah thought for a minute before saying, "Yeah, I guess it's okay," and heading to the bathroom down the hall.

Jackson walked around the bed and pulled Natalie to her feet, kissing her forehead. "That went well, *girlfriend*," he said as he held her.

"They adore you. So do I." Natalie stood on her tiptoes to give him a kiss and then turned to her dresser to grab some clothes before slipping into the bathroom. She came out a couple of minutes later in yoga pants and a T-shirt with her bun up high.

"I should get them some breakfast," she said. Jackson nodded and took his turn in the bathroom.

Cereal was usually a staple in her house, but with the early wake-up call, Natalie had time to cook some eggs and sausages. She was throwing some toast in the toaster when

Jackson came out, fresh from the shower and dressed for work.

"Something smells amazing," he proclaimed as he entered the kitchen.

"Help yourself. There's fresh coffee made, and there are eggs and sausages on the table. The toast will be done in just a minute." Before she'd finished talking, she was being spun around and Jackson's nose was buried in her neck.

"I wasn't talking about the food," he growled softly in her ear. "I want this every day: waking up next to you, breakfast with the kids, all of it."

"That sounds perfect." Natalie smiled. This was everything she'd ever wanted. Even the early days with Dave had never been like this. She didn't know if it was the mating bond forming or something else, but Natalie knew she was ready for Jackson to be a part of their lives.

"There's somewhere I want to take you and the kids. Can we go this weekend?" Jackson asked as they finished breakfast and he helped Natalie with the dishes.

Natalie frowned. "Dave has the kids this weekend. He'll get them after their soccer games Friday afternoon."

"Next weekend, then?"

"Next weekend sounds great."

Jackson got a twinkle in his eye. "So I'll have you to myself this weekend?"

Natalie smiled again and nodded.

Jackson kissed her deeply. "See you at work?"

"Are you sure about this, Jackson? We'll have to be professional. Patients won't think highly of you if they find their vet groping his office manager when they get to the exam room."

"I'm sure. I'll be on my best behavior. I promise."

"Okay, then. I'll get ready after I take the kids to school. Be there at ten?"

"See you then," he said with a big grin on his face. He gave Natalie another kiss, Emma a hug, and Noah a fist bump before moving toward the door.

"Jackson?" Natalie called out, stopping him in his tracks. He turned as he reached for the door.

"Yes, Natty?"

"Could you please explain things to Cheryl? She saw me looking a little disheveled coming out of your office yesterday. I don't want her to think poorly of me." The last thing she needed was to start a new job with everyone thinking she was a hussy.

"I'll make sure she knows how wonderful you are." Jackson winked and walked out the door.

Jackson

Jackson couldn't keep the smile off his face on his way to the office. He greeted Cheryl cheerfully. "Good morning, Cheryl!"

"Good morning, Doctor Lake. This sure is a change. I don't think I've seen a real smile since you took over."

"I had a good night's sleep." Best he had ever slept, actually. "Natalie Brooks, the woman I interviewed yesterday, will be starting as the office manager today. Please show her the ropes."

Cheryl's cheeks darkened and a small frown formed as she remembered who Natalie was. She raised an eyebrow at him in question.

Jackson raised his palms in the air. "Now, before you say anything, I want to disclose that she is my ma—girlfriend." He had almost said *mate*. "We were separated a month ago and were just reunited unexpectedly. Doc Jones had chosen her resume for an interview, and I had no idea she was here. Please don't let anything you may have seen yesterday sway your opinion of her. She's fully capable of the position."

"Sure, doctor," Cheryl replied, unconvinced. "Your first patient is on the way. A two-year-old boxer unraveled and ate a rug. And Mr. Anderson is bringing in one of his barn cats to be checked out—he thinks she might be pregnant."

"Thanks, Cheryl. I'll be in the back getting ready."

Mr. Anderson's cat was indeed very pregnant, and close to giving birth. He asked to leave her there in a kennel until the kittens arrived and the momma could be spayed. He also asked if Jackson would help find them homes when it was time.

The boxer's x-ray showed the unraveled braided wool rug blocking his intestines. He would require surgery. Jackson was checking the pre-op bloodwork when Natalie arrived.

He smelled her as soon as she walked into the clinic, despite the strong antiseptic scent that usually filled the building. Since their night together, her smell had intensified. He saw her briefly as Cheryl gave her a tour of the clinic. She gave a sweet little wave before Cheryl moved her along to the next room. He didn't see her again until lunch, when she knocked on the office door.

"I packed you a lunch," Natalie said, peeking her head through the half-open door.

He smiled, remembering the picnic they'd shared on their kayaking trip. "Come eat with me?"

Natalie returned the smile and entered the room with two paper bags. She'd packed him a couple of sandwiches, a bag of chips, and an apple. For herself, she had just one sandwich and an apple. She must have noticed his heavy appetite when he took thirds at dinner last night and again at breakfast this morning.

They ate their lunch and talked about their day. Natalie told him how Cheryl had been friendly as she showed her the clinic and introduced her to the phone system. After lunch, they were going to start on the scheduling software. Jackson told her about the mom-to-be and the operation he'd be performing on the boxer this afternoon.

His life had turned around so quickly. It was as if they'd never been apart at all. Talking with Natalie just felt natural.

When Natalie stood up to take care of the trash, Jackson grabbed her hand and pulled her onto his lap. One hand held her hip in place while the other hand gently pulled her face to his so he could kiss her.

"I thought you were going to behave yourself," Natalie stated in between kisses.

"Lunch doesn't count. Maybe if you didn't smell so good, I could wait, but I can't resist."

"What do I smell like? It must be pretty good for you to risk our integrity."

He moved his head to her neck and inhaled—not that he needed to. He'd never forget the smell that drove him wild.

"Strawberries and coconut. It's *divine*. And I would never do anything to hurt your integrity." Pulling back, he thought of a question. "What about me? Do I have a certain smell to you?"

Jackson didn't know what a human mate might experience with a shifter. The only mates he knew were his parents, and they didn't talk about it. Some things he'd caught onto growing up, like how they seemed to have conversations without speaking, or how his dad always knew how his mom was feeling, even if they were miles apart. But the more intimate details were a mystery.

Natalie thought for a moment. "Hmm...trees. Cedar and evergreen. Just like the forest where we met." Jackson smiled and gave her one more kiss before the bell on the entrance door rang.

"Lunch is over," Jackson said sadly. "I'll be in surgery for the rest of the afternoon. Can I join you again for dinner?"

"I wouldn't have it any other way."

Jackson and Natalie easily fell into a routine over the next few days, working alongside each other at the clinic and at home—sharing meals every day, and a bed every night, with lots of holding and kissing in between.

It wasn't without its hardships, though. It was becoming more and more challenging for Jackson to control himself with each passing day. Every touch from Natalie made him want her more.

On their third night together, Jackson had just given Natalie a dose of the pleasure she enjoyed so much. He'd kept control this time—barely. She relaxed beside him with her fingers drawing little pictures on his chest and abdomen. She looked up at him with her sleepy eyes and shocked him when she dropped her hand and wrapped it around him through his shorts.

"Natty..." he moaned, his voice going gravelly.

"You've taken care of me. I think it's about time I return the favor." She started rubbing his length, giving his balls a gentle squeeze when she reached the base. Before she made it up to the tip, a scream let out down the hall. Jackson groaned as Natalie hopped out of bed.

"That's Noah," she said as she bolted out of the room. Jackson took a couple of minutes to take some deep breaths before following Natalie. It didn't take his erection long to recede once worry began to fill him from the scream.

When he got to Noah's room, Natalie was lying beside her son on his bed. Noah was crying as he described his nightmare. "It was the wolves again, Mom. There were two and the one was snarling and snapping and I was so scared."

Natalie looked up at Jackson standing in the doorway.

"I think I need to tell him, Natty." She nodded her head and he sat on the end of Noah's bed. "Hey there, champ. When we were in the woods, did you by chance open your eyes when I told you to keep them closed?"

Noah bowed his head, ashamed for not following directions. "I tried to keep them closed but I couldn't. I opened them just for a second and I saw...I thought I saw two wolves. I closed them again, and when I opened them, the wolves were gone and you were there to take me home." Panic filled his voice, his posture, and his scent. It stirred concern and worry in Jackson. *So this is what it feels like to be a parent.*

Natalie looked at Jackson in shock. "He truly did see a wolf in the woods?"

"I didn't tell you because I wasn't sure what he saw. I should have, and I'm sorry." Jackson knew he'd pay for that oversight later, but for now, he looked at Noah. "Champ, when you opened your eyes, you did see two wolves. I was the second wolf. I'm what's called a wolf shifter. The other wolf was also a shifter. I had to turn into my wolf so I could talk to him, since he wouldn't shift to talk to me."

Jackson squeezed Noah's foot in comfort. "He wasn't snarling at you—he was snarling because he sensed me and he didn't want him to hurt you. Once I told him who I was, he ran off and I shifted back."

Noah shot off a string of questions so fast as his breathing picked up. "You're a werewolf? Are you going to bite me? Did you bite Mom? Are we all going to be werewolves?"

"Not a werewolf—a wolf shifter. We can talk about the differences later, but no, I'm not going to bite you, and you wouldn't turn into anything if I did. Being a wolf shifter is like...it's like having superpowers, just like in your comics."

Noah's panic was replaced with surprise and wonder at the mention of superheroes. "You can really turn into a wolf? Can I see?"

"Some other time, but not tonight," Jackson answered gently. "I just want you to know that there's nothing to worry about. No one was or is going to hurt you. You're safe. But you can't tell anybody what I am, okay, champ? Most people don't know about shifters and not everyone would be happy about it." Noah just nodded. Jackson could almost see the questions that were whirling behind his sleepy eyes.

"We can talk about this more tomorrow. It's late and you have school in the morning," Natalie said as she tucked Noah's blankets up around him. "Think you can get back to sleep?"

"Yeah, Mom. Thanks for telling me, Jackson. I promise I won't tell anyone."

"Thanks, champ. Good night." Jackson let his eyes glow and Noah's eyes grew wide in wonder. Jackson smiled and took Natalie's hand while she said goodnight, then he led her down the hall to her bedroom.

Chapter Twenty-Two

Natalie

Jackson had barely shut and locked the door when Natalie squared on him.

"Why didn't you tell me about the wolf? Noah has been having these nightmares since we came home. It would have been nice to know that it was real."

"I'm sorry, Natty. It was dark and I didn't know what he saw. I didn't know how to explain it in front of...everyone."

"You need to tell me these things, Jackson. Especially when it comes to my kids." Natalie sighed and sat down on the bed, rubbing her hand down her face. "Maybe this is all just happening too fast." She wasn't angry. Not really. They were just getting used to each other—she couldn't expect Jackson to just jump right into parenting. She didn't even know if he wanted to.

"No, Natty. Please don't say that," Jackson pleaded. He knelt in front of her, taking her hands. "I just got you back. I can't be without you again. Ever."

"It's not just me, Jackson. I have two kids that just had

their world split apart, and even though they said they're okay with us, it's still happening really fast. There's so much we still don't know about each other. Do you even want to be a dad? Do you want a family, or do you just want me?"

"Natalie." Jackson turned serious. "I *love* your kids. I love how smart Noah is. I love that an eagle could land in front of him and lay a golden egg that hatches into a dragon, and he wouldn't look up from his comics. And yet he's still so in tune with the feelings of those around him. And Emma—that girl could talk my ear off for hours and I'd never get tired of it. Of course, I want to be their dad. I want you. I want a family. I want it all."

Jackson paused, and Natalie waited for the "but..." However, when he spoke again, it wasn't what Natalie expected.

"If we need to...slow it down, I can go home right now. We can talk on the phone, go on dates, and I can kiss you goodnight at the door. It might be the second hardest thing I've ever done, but I'll do it. I'd wait forever for you, Natty."

A tear fell down Natalie's cheek and Jackson immediately wiped it away. He started to stand to leave, but she grabbed his hands to stop him. The thought of him leaving made her chest clench in panic.

"No, Jackson, don't go. But in the future, I need to know everything when it comes to my kids."

"I know. I'll make sure to tell you all the things from here on out." His arms reached for her and she moved into him, wrapping her arms around his waist.

"Wait—you said going slow would've been the second hardest thing. What was the first?"

"Letting you drive away from that campground." He placed a gentle kiss on her lips before pulling away.

"Look at us—we made it through our first argument," Natalie said, grinning at him.

"Does that mean we get to make up?" Jackson dipped his head again and she leaned into his kiss. In a single movement, she was swept off her feet and onto the bed and her shorts had disappeared. Jackson pulled her to the edge of the bed and rubbed her feet as he started kissing her ankles.

"Jackson, I was supposed to be taking care of you."

"Shhh, beautiful. I have an apology to make."

Jackson

Jackson moved upward, trailing kisses up each leg, spending extra time when he got to her inner thigh. As he got nearer to her crease, he sensed some nerves from her. When he planted a kiss right in the center of her wet panties, he felt her heart rate spike. He moved up to place a kiss on her lips and to look in her eyes.

"Natty, I want to taste you."

She contemplated for a moment before nodding and dropping her head back, her eyes closed. "Okay."

Jackson removed her top and started another trail of kisses from her lips straight down to her belly button. A swirl around her belly button earned him a pleasure-filled groan.

When Jackson got to the edge of her panties, he hooked a finger on either side and started to work them down her hips. She lifted enough for him to get them over and off her legs. He moved in between her legs, pushing her knees apart to open her up. His hands rubbed her thighs as he dropped his kisses to her center. Natalie gasped as he licked and kissed along her folds. Her heart rate was sky-high, but so was the smell of her arousal.

Jackson moaned at the taste of his mate. She was just as sweet as he imagined. He took his time licking and kissing his way to her clit. When he sucked on the sensitive knot, Natalie arched her back with the sweetest little moan.

He continued to work her until she was near her peak. Instead of taking her over the edge, he backed off and teased her entrance. She wiggled in complaint as she tried to get him to move where she wanted him.

"Not yet, beautiful," Jackson said as his hands moved to hold her legs in place while he continued to lap around her entrance and up and down her folds.

Just when he'd made her believe he was moving toward her clit, he inserted a finger through her slick entrance. She whimpered as he ran his finger along the edges of the canal.

"Please, Jackson," she pleaded.

He slipped in and out a couple of times before adding a second finger. As he curled them into her sweet spot, he moved his lips to her clit and sucked hard. Her back arched and her hips bucked as she fell apart. He continued kissing and lapping up her juices until her tremors settled.

One last kiss to her swollen lower lips and he closed her knees and moved up to where Natalie lay with her eyes closed, quietly panting.

"Are you okay, Natty?" Jackson asked. He'd felt her nerves lessen as he went along, but he was still worried that he took things too far.

"Yes. That was...It's just...I've never...N*o one* has ever..." Natalie struggled to get her words out.

"No one has ever gone down on you?" She shook her head and he understood her nerves. He brushed the hair out of her face and kissed her forehead. "And? How do you feel about it?"

Natalie turned her bright blue eyes toward him. A slow smile grew on her face. Her eyes sparked and she said, "Do it again?"

Jackson laughed and started his trail of kisses back down her body.

Chapter Twenty-Three

Natalie

Natalie awoke with Jackson wrapped around her, the room cooled by the chilly fall air outside. It was still dark out as the days grew shorter. Even though morning came too soon, Natalie was content and happy. Jackson had brought her to climax two more times in the night.

Natalie'd had more orgasms in the last few days than she had in *years* with Dave, and she and Jackson hadn't even had sex yet. Dave was her first and it had always been about him.

Jackson's desire to please her first surprised her. When he asked to taste her, her nerves went haywire. Despite being married for ten years and having two kids, Natalie felt she was relatively sexually inexperienced. She had a feeling that was about to change—and she wasn't complaining.

Friday afternoon came and Natalie left work early to get the kids to their soccer games. Lacey had driven up to watch the kids play and was meeting them at the fields. Natalie hadn't seen much of her best friend since the new semester started, and she was excited to see her and tell her about Jackson. She was watching Noah's warmups when Lacey walked up.

"You look happy. What's going on?" Lacey asked as she wrapped Natalie in a big hug.

"Well, you remember the guy from camping I told you about? Jackson?"

"The sexy park ranger? Yes, I remember."

"He lives here...and he's my boss."

Lacey squealed, releasing Natalie and jumping ecstatically. "No way! *Please* tell me he's more than your boss."

Just then, a strong pair of arms wrapped around Natalie's waist in a way that was becoming amazingly normal. She didn't have to look to know who it was. Lacey squealed again, giving Jackson a once-over, and showed Natalie a sign of approval.

Natalie laughed at her friend as she made introductions. "Lacey, this is Jackson."

"Nice to finally meet you, Lacey. Natalie has told me a lot about you."

"Likewise," Lacey said before she moved her gaze across the field and scowled. "Uh, Nat..." she muttered and nodded her head to draw Natalie's attention.

Dave was approaching the other sideline, a scowl on his face. He paused as he took in the sight of his ex-wife in the arms of another man. Natalie lifted her hand in a small, friendly wave. Dave stood still and Natalie prepared herself for an argument. As she expected, he marched across the field, right through the kids chaotically kicking balls toward the goal, and straight up to Natalie.

"You cheating slut!" Dave spat, his finger pointed and shaking in her face. "I tried to reconcile. Took you to show you off to my bosses. This whole time, you were lying and screwing the campground janitor? How could you? I gave you everything."

Jackson moved himself between Natalie and Dave. He grabbed Dave's hand and tried to lower it out of her face.

"Look, man, this isn't the place. There are kids around," Jackson said calmly, trying to diffuse the situation.

"Get your hands off me!" Dave shouted as he yanked his hand away. "You left me for this loser? What can he give you that I didn't? Look at you—you're a mess."

Natalie thought about her appearance. Her curls were thrown into her favorite messy bun and stuck through the hole of her ball cap, her light makeup wearing off after a day at work. She wore her favorite leggings and T-shirt under a light jacket. She wasn't dressed to the nines, but she was hardly a mess. It was a soccer game, for goodness sake.

"Don't listen to him. You look perfect," Jackson told her softly. "You don't have to take this."

That was all Natalie needed to find her backbone. She wasn't married to Dave anymore. She didn't need to answer to him, and she certainly didn't need to listen to him talk to her that way. She stepped out from behind Jackson and took his hand for support. Just being near him gave her strength.

"You think you gave me everything, Dave? You gave me *nothing*, and you took everything. You treated me like your prize and not your wife. You put your needs in front of everyone else. You never asked what I wanted, what I needed, what I liked or disliked. You don't get to come here, to my home, and accuse me in front of *everyone* of cheating. I never cheated on you, Dave. But you? You cheated me out of ten years of my life. The only good thing to come out of our marriage are those kids out there." Natalie gestured toward Noah, huddled with his team listening to their coach, and to Emma, sitting in the grass picking dandelions.

"As for reconciling, you drove five hours, told me how much of an embarrassment I was, accused me of cheating, left me to pack up on my own, and then expected me to come to a banquet that same day," she continued. "Not to mention, you served me with divorce papers less than forty-eight hours later. You had no intention of coming home."

Natalie let go of Jackson's hand and his arm immediately went around her. "I didn't leave you, Dave—you left me, and now I've moved on. You need to move on too, and start thinking about what's best for your kids for once in your life. Standing here calling their mother names—that isn't it."

Natalie turned away and pulled Jackson over to where Lacey had been watching. She spread out a blanket and sat down with Lacey joining her. Jackson waited until Dave sulked over to the bleachers on the other side of the field and then laid down on his side, pulling Natalie to lean against his chest while they watched.

Noah was the fastest kid on his team and scored two goals in his game. He gave his dad a wave before he joined Natalie on the blanket. Dave didn't wave back—he was too busy staring at his phone. Jackson gave Noah a fist bump and said, "Well done, champ!" which made him smile.

Emma had them all laughing as she sat down in the middle of the goal halfway through the game and started picking blades of grass. When Emma's game was done, Lacey took off to school and Jackson escorted Natalie and the kids to the parking lot to meet up with Dave.

Noah was more hesitant with his dad than Emma. He hung back with Natalie while Emma ran to her dad.

"Daddy! Daddy! We're coming to your house for the weekend!"

"Yes, Emma, we just have to get your things. Go grab

your stuff while I talk to your mom," Dave said flatly. Noah took Emma's hand and took her over to Natalie's car to grab their bags.

This time, instead of addressing Natalie, Dave turned to Jackson. "Listen, these are *my* children. If you think you can just sweep in and take them like you took my wife, you're mistaken."

"Dave!" Natalie scolded. "Nobody said anything about taking the kids from you. I want nothing more than for you to spend time with them. Can we please be civil about this?"

"Fine," Dave hissed. "Go clean yourself up, Lee. You look like crap."

Natalie couldn't hold Jackson back this time. She heard a low growl as he took two long steps toward Dave until he towered over her ex. "You will not speak to her like that."

Dave took an involuntary step back, eyes seething. He shook his head and turned toward his car as the kids approached with their bags. "This isn't over," he spat as he opened his trunk.

Natalie took Jackson's hand and anxiously moved closer, pulling their hands behind them when she saw his claws were starting to come out. She rubbed his hand with her thumb until they retracted again. Only then did Natalie let go of his hand and turn to the kids.

Natalie and Jackson both gave the kids hugs goodbye before they climbed into the overly fancy vehicle. She made sure they were both safely buckled before closing their doors and turning away.

"Oh, and Dave?" Natalie called out, unable to resist. "You should probably get some botox. I think I see a wrinkle."

Natalie turned away as Dave got in his car. She didn't

feel a bit of remorse for anything that had happened, knowing that the man she'd married at nineteen was completely gone. The truth was that she didn't miss him at all.

She was always meant to be with Jackson. She just wished she'd met him first, before Dave caused them all so much heartache.

Jackson

Jackson had nearly lost control as Dave verbally attacked his mate. Only Natalie's calming presence as she rubbed his hand had kept him from shifting further and lunging at Dave.

Natalie buried her face in Jackson's shirt as Dave and the kids drove away. Tears were streaming down her face. "Natty, honey, what's wrong?"

"I just miss them already. I've never been away from them before."

"Oh, my beautiful mate, the weekend will be over before you know it." He rubbed her back and her sobs settled. "Dave was a little unhinged. Are you sure he's never hurt you?"

"Physically, no, he's never hurt me. The Dave I knew—the Dave I married—I thought was a decent guy. I thought it was just a case of us getting married too young. If we'd taken more time, maybe we would have seen that we wanted different things. Now I see all the red flags I should have seen before. This Dave—I don't know this Dave at all."

Jackson kissed away her tears. He hated to see them on her face. Hated that she had something to be sad about. "I'd like to show you something. Feeling up to it?"

Natalie wiped away one last tear. "Of course."

They dropped off her car at her house and Jackson opened the passenger door to his truck for her. He folded up the console so she could sit close and he put his arm around her. He knew having to split time with her kids was hard on her, but he was happy to have her to himself for a little bit. They rode in quiet contentment until he pulled onto a gravel drive.

Natalie sat up as she saw a white picket fence surrounding pastures on either side of the drive. Just past the small pastures, the drive split. The right drive went toward a barn and a large backyard. The left, to a yellow-sided house with white trim and a big wraparound porch. Her eyes widened and her left hand clasped his knee. "Oh, Jackson..."

"Welcome home, Natty."

"This is *yours*?"

Jackson nodded as he parked the truck. "I knew as soon as I saw it that I had to buy it. I didn't think I'd ever see you again, but I wanted to think of us here. I wanted to sit on the porch and picture you in a field of goats or in the front yard with your belly round and full with my baby. I wanted to see Emma riding her pony around the pasture. I wanted Noah on the porch swing reading those comics he loves. Even if it was all in my imagination."

Natalie climbed up onto her knees and wrapped her arms around his neck. "It doesn't have to be in your imagination anymore." She kissed him and his heart was about to burst. She was right. He could have all those things now that she was here by his side.

"Would you like to see inside?"

"Yes!" Natalie exclaimed excitedly. Jackson opened the truck door and pulled her through his side, lifting her out as if she were a feather. They walked hand in hand up the front steps and onto the porch. He unlocked the door and they stepped into an open foyer with an elegant but rustic chandelier.

"Something smells amazing," Natalie observed.

"I put a roast in the slow cooker for dinner. I hope you like it."

"You cooked me dinner?" Tears welled in her eyes again. She blinked them away, but Jackson could guess that no one had ever cooked for her. She put everything into taking care of others. He was going to make sure he took care of her.

Chapter Twenty-Four

Natalie

When Jackson pulled up the gravel drive to his house, Natalie couldn't believe her eyes. She was looking at her dream home. It was the very image of the house she'd described to Jackson on their hike. How he had managed to find it, and afford it, she didn't know.

He walked her through the foyer and into the open-concept living room and kitchen. The living room had a big sectional situated around a stone fireplace. A large television was mounted over the mantle, perfect for watching movies on cold winter nights.

Between the living room and kitchen was a large table that was perfect for holidays and family dinners. The kitchen was beautiful, with granite countertops and updated appliances. On the end of the kitchen was a bay window with a small breakfast nook for more intimate meals.

After the kitchen, Jackson took her down the hallway to

the bedrooms. On the right was a guest bedroom with an attached bathroom. Next to the guest room was an office, complete with mahogany desk and bookshelf-lined walls. On the left were two rooms with a bathroom between them. One room was pink, one was blue, each with a loft bed with a desk underneath. Natalie looked at Jackson in surprise. *Did he make up these rooms for my kids?*

As if he could read her thoughts, Jackson stated, "It was painted like this when I bought it and the furniture was included. I thought it would be perfect for Emma and Noah. They can decorate it however they want. We can paint them, too, if they don't like the colors."

Natalie just stared at him in awe.

Lastly, Jackson opened the door to the master suite. The wall across from the door was covered in floor-to-ceiling windows that faced the woods. Pretty sheer curtains hung on each one for privacy. She couldn't imagine anyone being on this side of the house, though, and pictured lying in bed with Jackson and enjoying the view. She'd love to watch the rain fall out the windows, or make love in a thunderstorm with only the lightning through the windows lighting up the room. That thought surprised her, since she had asked him to take things slow. But after Dave's performance, and now, standing here in her dream house with her dream guy, she didn't think that mattered as much anymore.

Three doorways filled the far wall of the bedroom. One was a huge walk-in closet that was hardly filled. In the middle was a set of French doors draped in more sheer curtains. On the other side was a single door to the master bath, complete with a jacuzzi tub.

"What's in there?" Natalie asked, pointing to the French doors. Jackson opened them and Natalie walked into the most whimsically decorated nursery. A rocking chair sat in the corner and a stunning white crib with a matching changing table and dresser lined the walls. It even had its own little closet.

"I never asked if you wanted more kids," Jackson said softly. "I understand if you don't. But if you do..." He trailed off. Natalie thought she sensed a bit of hope in his voice and she remembered the comment he made earlier, about her belly in the field of goats. "I asked the realtor to include the staging furniture, which I guess included this too, but we can get whatever you'd like. Or we can turn this into an office for you, or a craft room. Whatever you want, Natty—I'll be happy."

"It's perfect, Jackson. I'd be honored to have a baby with you someday."

Jackson swung her up and twirled her around. "I love you, Natty," he said as he lowered her to her feet and caught her lips in a kiss.

They had been together for such a short amount of time. She'd dated Dave for months before either of them said *I love you*. But here, in this moment, after only five days, those three little words were exactly what Natalie wanted to hear.

"I love you too, Jackson." He swept her up again, this time depositing her on the king-size bed, kissing her frantically.

"What about dinner?" she asked as he lavished kisses from one ear around to the other. He lifted his head, his eyes smoldering into hers.

"Are you hungry, Natty?"

She shook her head. She wasn't hungry. Not for dinner, anyway.

His possessive lips met hers, claiming them and melding together with so much passion. She moaned a little as his tongue teased hers. A rush of heat pooled between her thighs. Natalie reached down to the hem of his shirt and rolled it up over his muscled chest. She had longed to run her hands over those muscles since she saw them for the first time while camping. Jackson took one hand and pulled his shirt the rest of the way over his head.

He then took her hands and pulled her up to sit on the edge of the bed. Her shirt quickly joined his on the floor. He moved down, removing one of her shoes and then the other. She lifted her hips and he pulled her pants and her panties off in one slick move. He knelt down and kissed up one leg and down the other. At her apex, he paused to give a couple of licks while his hand reached up to unsnap her bra. She sat in front of him completely naked.

Jackson looked up at her with eyes filled with desire. "You're so beautiful."

She felt exposed and yet yearned for it at the same time. Every stretch mark, every scar, every flaw was in front of him, and yet Jackson was still enamored with her. He'd called her beautiful since the day they met, and here, in this moment, she believed it.

Natalie rested on her elbows and let her head tilt back, her knees falling to the side, inviting Jackson forward. He growled and began devouring her like a starved wolf. She lifted her head, wanting to see the reaction she had on him, only to see that his eyes were glowing green. His animal was close to the surface and that unexpectedly excited her.

"Oh, my wolf, please don't stop," she begged.

Jackson looked at her with a wolfish grin as he inserted first one finger, then another, before lowering his head back down. She couldn't hold herself up for long when he got to her throbbing clit. He licked, kissed, and sucked her while his fingers worked until she fell over the edge in ecstasy. He continued kissing, lapping her center until the stars cleared from her eyes.

Jackson got off his knees in an attempt to join her on the bed, but Natalie sat up and stopped him before he could. "Not so fast."

She grabbed the front pockets of his jeans to pull him closer so she could undo his button and zipper. Jackson had spent so much time restraining himself over the last week—he'd barely let her touch him. She was done waiting. She carefully pulled his jeans over his erection and they dropped to the floor. She reached for his boxers and he growled a warning, gripping her wrists. "Natalie..." He rarely used her full name. "I don't have much control."

She looked up at him innocently and said, "Jackson, I want to taste you," mimicking what he'd told her the other night.

His eyes smoldered, glowing even brighter, and he released her wrists, allowing her to ease down his boxers. She wrapped her small hand around him and licked the underside of his hard shaft. She swirled her tongue around the tip, taking in the bead of pre-cum that had formed. He groaned when she took him fully into her mouth.

Natalie loved that she could make him come undone. He'd been so good to her; getting her chance to do the same for him turned her on even more. She moved in tandem with her hand, meeting in the middle, licking and sucking as she increased her pace. He throbbed in her mouth. She was ready to swallow every bit of his essence when he grabbed her hair and tenderly pulled her off him.

"Natalie, I'm so close. I can't promise I can stop." She

only nodded. "Natty, I need you to tell me what you want. Tell me what you need, beautiful."

Her need pulsed everywhere within Natalie. She knew what she wanted and it certainly wasn't stopping. She was ready for all of him. She was ready to take one giant leap and bind herself to this amazing man forever.

"Jackson. I want…I *need* you inside me. I need you to bite me."

Jackson

Natalie had barely gotten the words out when Jackson nudged her back onto the bed. He climbed in between her legs, spreading her wide. Reaching between them, he stroked her a few times, swirling the tip of his finger around her entrance to make sure she was ready for him. It was unnecessary. She was dripping wet for him. He leaned down to capture her lips in his.

He'd been waiting for this moment. Waiting to make her his. Each day he couldn't mark her felt like a decade. Now she was here, a beautiful goddess lying before him, offering herself to him. To be his. Forever.

As they kissed, Jackson moved toward her entrance. He slid inside her, stretching and filling her. His name escaped her lips as a mere gasp. He'd never tire of hearing it. He gave her a moment to adjust to him before pulling out all but the tip and plunging back in. He moved a couple more times before her hips moved to join him. They moved in perfect rhythm—not too fast, not too slow. When he felt the pressure reaching its peak, he reached between them and pinched her clit. When her tremors started, he found the spot where her neck met her shoulder and let his fangs sink in.

Natalie screamed in pleasure to match his howl as they came together. The complete bliss that he felt was more than he could have ever imagined. He knew the bond was intense, but there was nothing that could compare. He felt every ounce of her pleasure as well as his own. It was the most intense feeling he had ever felt. He felt like it might break him in two and make him whole at the same time.

Jackson let his fangs remain in her skin until their bodies relaxed. He licked the bite clean and kissed it, which sent a shudder through Natalie. *Mine. My mate.*

"That was incredible," Natalie breathed.

"You are incredible," Jackson replied. He rolled off her and pulled her against him, peppering her with kisses. "I'm sorry, Natalie. I know you wanted to go slow. I just needed you."

"Jackson. Quit apologizing. I needed you, too. Slow was never going to work for us. It was perfect. You are perfect. I love you."

"I love you too, my beautiful mate. How do you feel?"

"I feel...whole," Natalie responded. Jackson couldn't have described it better. He had everything that had ever been missing in his life. He knew whatever happened now, he had Natalie. He had his family. And anything else was just a bonus.

"Is it too soon for me to ask you to move in with me?" Jackson asked hopefully.

"Probably. But who cares? I don't ever want to spend a night without you. Of course, I'll move in."

Jackson kissed her again. Even this simple kiss was different—more intense, as he could feel her emotions as well as his own. He felt himself getting hard again until he heard her stomach growl. She giggled and said, "I guess I am hungry now."

"Let's go eat that dinner."

Chapter Twenty-Five

Natalie

They spent the weekend talking, making plans, and making love all over their new home. Natalie felt like a new person. The spot where Jackson had bit her was completely healed by morning, with only a small scar remaining. Flowing from her mark was what felt like a tether, tying her forever to her mate. She could sense his emotions through the bond even more than before, and the cedar and evergreen scent that she had associated with him was even stronger. Neither one of them knew how much her body might change after being mated to a wolf, though she would never fully shift.

All the fears and doubts Natalie had in herself disappeared the moment the mating bond snapped into place. She knew that here, with Jackson, was where she was meant to be. Her body craved his touch and her heart, his company. The fact that she had gotten divorced only a week ago didn't even matter. That marriage was never meant to be. Everything just made sense now, in a way she couldn't explain.

On Sunday morning, they watched the sun rise out their bedroom window after Jackson woke her as he gently entered her from behind. He slowly and tenderly rocked her to a long, drawn-out orgasm before letting go of his own release.

"Natty." He spoke her name with concern in his voice. "We've been going at it like rabbits and haven't used a bit of protection. I don't think you're in heat, but I can't be sure."

She turned to face him. *Only a vet would say in heat.* Getting pregnant didn't bother her. While she'd like some time just to be with Jackson, and for the kids to adjust to yet another sudden change in their lives, she knew it was a road they were headed down sooner or later.

"Maybe we'll be filling that nursery after all." Natalie smiled.

Jackson smiled back and kissed her deeply. "In that case, maybe we need some more practice."

"Down, boy." Natalie chuckled. "We have to get ready to meet the kids." Spending the weekend with Jackson had been incredible, and it had helped keep her mind busy, but she missed her kids and was ready for them to come home.

Natalie was quiet as they drove to her house to meet Dave and the kids. How was she going to tell her ex-husband, who she divorced only a week ago, that she was moving in with the guy she started dating before the ink on the divorce papers had dried? Before Jackson, she would have thought anyone in her situation was insane. Even now, she wondered if she was in a dream. But when she accepted the reality of it all, she realized that they may have made it official only a week ago, but their marriage had been over long before.

Dave wasn't due until the afternoon, so Natalie and Jackson cozied up on the couch and talked more about the plans for their new home. While Jackson had bought the staging furniture from the realtor, he told Natalie that he had only done it because he didn't care about the furniture unless he was choosing it with her. They talked about what to keep and what to replace, which paint colors they liked, and even what animals they would get first. Jackson wanted goats to fulfill his fantasy, and Natalie wanted cats, mostly to get a rise out of Jackson. Her plan worked and he tackled her to the couch, finding all her ticklish spots.

His tickles started turning into kisses until Natalie's phone rang. An unknown number lit up her screen.

"Hello?" Natalie answered.

"Hi, Natalie? This is Ashley, Dave's secretary."

"What do you need, Ashley?" Natalie asked hesitantly. She didn't know why her ex-husband's secretary would be calling her.

"Umm...Dave asked me to call you and tell you..." Ashley paused, her voice wavering slightly. "He wanted me to tell you that your son, uh, Nick...? He's missing."

"Noah is *missing*?" Natalie shouted, jumping up from the couch. "What do you mean, he's missing? Why are *you* calling me? Where is Dave?"

"Uh...He said the babysitter called and said the kid was missing, so he asked me to call you while he drove home?"

Babysitter? Natalie's pulse spiked as she began shaking. "Drove home from *where*, Ashley?" she asked through gritted teeth.

"The office?" The girl answered everything like a question.

"I'm on my way," Natalie said, hanging up before Ashley could say anything else.

Jackson

With his shifter hearing, Jackson had heard the entire conversation as the blundering woman on the phone informed Natalie that her son was missing. He had already grabbed her jacket, her purse, and his keys, and was ushering her out the door when she hung up the phone.

"Tell me where to go," Jackson stated as they got into his truck. Through their mate bond, he felt the storm of emotions more strongly than he had before. Natalie's rage and fear were almost enough to make him shift to hunt down Dave. Something about this guy was making him lose the control over his animal he had so carefully built.

He put the address into his GPS and took off down the gravel driveway.

Once they were on their way, Jackson took Natalie's hand and held it tight. "It's going to be okay. We'll find Noah."

"I just can't believe him," Natalie cried. "He has them for one weekend and he can't even keep out of the office. Who's supposed to be watching the kids?" Her eyes grew wide. "Emma! Who's with Emma?"

Jackson's own fury brewed, on top of everything radiating from Natalie, and he drove faster. He already considered Noah a son and was desperate to find him.

They arrived at Dave's apartment building and Natalie hastily led him through the front doors and to the elevator.

When the doors on the elevator closed, Jackson pulled Natalie close. "We'll find him. Maybe he's just hiding."

Natalie just nodded, shaking as she tried to hold in her sobs. As soon as the elevator stopped, she was out the doors before they fully opened with Jackson close behind. She blew into Dave's apartment like a hurricane. Dave wasn't there and the door hadn't even been locked. Jackson surveyed the place as Natalie ran to Emma, who was engrossed in the cartoon she was watching, and pulled her into her arms. There were no pictures, no toys or books, nothing at all to make it feel like a home, especially to children.

"What's wrong, Mommy?" Emma asked, not understanding the severity of the situation. As Natalie seemed to have trouble speaking, Jackson took charge.

"Hey, little duck, do you know where your brother is?"

"No." Emma shrugged. "He left."

"Did he say where he was going? Did anyone go with him?" Jackson pushed further.

"No. Daddy left for work and said Erica was going to watch us. Noah just told me to stay here and he left."

"Who is Erica?"

"She lives across the hall," Emma said nonchalantly.

It was then that Jackson noticed the teenage girl sitting on the couch, twirling her hair and glued to her phone. She hadn't even noticed them come in. He cleared his throat loudly to get her attention. When she didn't look up, he moved right in front of her and took the phone from her hands.

"*Hey!* Give that back!" she shouted before looking to see who took her phone. "Uh, who are you?"

"My name is Jackson. I'm here with Noah's mom. Do you know where he is?"

"Nope. I went to get them breakfast and then he was gone."

"And you don't see a problem with that?" Natalie chimed in, having found her voice. "Aren't you supposed to be watching him?"

The girl, Erica, just shrugged. "I called Mr. Evans."

"How long ago?" Jackson asked shortly.

"I dunno. An hour, maybe?" Erica said as she grabbed her phone from Jackson.

"An *hour!*" Natalie cried. "Ashley didn't call until thirty minutes ago, Jackson, and he's been missing over an hour? And where's Dave? Ashley said he was driving home. He should be here by now!"

"I know, honey," Jackson said as he rubbed her back. "You stay here with Emma and check the other rooms. I'll start looking outside. Is there any place he might have gone?"

"I—I don't know. Our old apartment, maybe? Or the park? He could be anywhere." Natalie dropped into a chair at the kitchen table, her head in her hands. Jackson hated to leave her alone and panicked, but someone needed to stay with Emma.

"Call Lacey and see if she can come sit with you. I'll let you know as soon as I find him."

Before he left, Jackson pulled a twenty-dollar bill out of his wallet and tossed it to Erica. "Here, for your troubles. You can leave now."

She pocketed the money and walked out the door. Jackson followed, opening his shifter senses. He followed Noah's scent to the elevator and into the lobby, where he ran into Dave.

"What are you doing here?" Dave asked when he saw Jackson.

"I'm looking for your son, who you don't seem to be too concerned about," Jackson spat back. He was done letting this jerk hurt his family.

"I had an important meeting. I can't reschedule things every time the kid decides to run off. I'm sure he'll be back soon."

Jackson couldn't believe what he was hearing. This guy had no care whatsoever that his child was missing. Jackson didn't want Dave anywhere near Natalie right now. He would only upset her with his lackadaisical attitude. He squared his shoulders and moved closer to Dave.

"Natalie is in your apartment with Emma. You will not go near her. You will not speak to her. You can go look for Noah, or you can stay down here, or go back to work, for all I care. But you will not go inside your apartment until I get back. Do you understand?"

"Who do you think you are, telling me what to do?" Dave retorted.

Jackson didn't have any more time to waste. He needed to find Noah. "You can stay out of your apartment, or I can call the police and report you for child endangerment," Jackson threatened. Dave said nothing, but walked out the front door, shaking his head and muttering under his breath.

Jackson went outside and began to search for Noah's scent trail again, but there were too many scents in the city. He couldn't shift with all the people around, so he started toward the address Natalie gave him for their old apartment. He stretched his senses as far as he could for any sign of Noah. While driving would have been faster, Noah would be on foot, and Jackson didn't want to miss anything.

When he got to the apartment, he finally picked up a trace of Noah. He had been there, but not for long. His scent went left, toward the park Natalie said they frequented. It took Jackson only minutes to get there, where he found Noah sitting at the top of a lookout tower that was built for the kids.

Jackson shot a quick text to Natalie before he climbed up and took a seat next to Noah. "Hey there, champ."

"Jackson? You found me?" Noah asked in surprise.

"Of course I did," Jackson replied matter-of-factly. "Your mom *may* have told me where to look," he added with a wink. "Do you want to tell me what's going on?"

Noah didn't answer at first. Jackson waited patiently until Noah spoke again, quiet as a mouse. "I didn't want to be at my dad's."

"Did something happen, Noah?"

"Nothing bad. He just wasn't there. He worked every day. When he *was* there, he was on the phone and we had to be quiet. There's nothing to do. When Emma asked him if he had any toys, he just told her toys are a waste of money. He ordered pizza with pineapple on it." Noah made a disgusted face. "I don't ever want to go back there. Can't you just be our dad?"

Jackson's heart warmed at the thought. "I would be honored to be a bonus dad for you, but your dad is still your dad. He loves you, even if he has things a little backward right now. And though I understand how you feel, leaving the apartment on your own was really dangerous."

"But you found me."

"I will always find you, champ. But it would be a lot easier on your mom and me if you would stop running and just talk to us instead."

Noah looked down at his feet. "I just get this feeling, when I'm mad, or scared, that I need to run."

Jackson knew the feeling well. The overwhelming desire to let his paws hit the dirt and leave everything behind. "You know, the day you and your mom and sister left the campground, I was so sad that I ran for two days. I got lost in the woods and had to find my way home."

"Really?" Noah asked in surprise.

"Really," Jackson responded. He felt his bond with the boy grow exponentially. "But I'm a grown-up, and even though you are the smartest nine-year-old I know, running away was not safe. You could have gotten really hurt or lost."

"I know," Noah said solemnly.

"How about this—when you get that urge to run, you tell me and we'll run together. And if I'm not around, you call me and we'll talk it through, okay?"

"Yeah, okay. Thanks, Jackson."

"Now, let's head back to your mom before she paces a hole in the floor."

Noah got a panicked look on his face. "Please don't tell my mom. I don't want her and my dad to fight again."

Jackson remembered his promise to Natalie, but he didn't want to break Noah's trust. He thought about his words carefully before answering, "I know you don't like it when your mom and dad argue, but we can't keep things from the people we love. You need to tell your mom how you feel, and I'll be right there to help you."

Noah looked defeated. Jackson didn't want to lose all the progress he felt he'd made, but he couldn't keep this from Natalie. Maybe he could make it more comfortable for Noah.

"Let's go talk to your mom, and then I'll take you and Emma for a walk while she talks to your dad. How does that sound?"

Noah nodded and he and Jackson climbed down from the lookout and started toward Dave's apartment.

Chapter Twenty-Six

Natalie

Natalie was pacing the floor when someone knocked on the door. Her first thought was that Dave had come home, and she wasn't ready to deal with him, but then she realized he probably wouldn't knock on his own door. She looked through the peephole and flung open the door when she saw Lacey.

"Any word yet?" Lacey asked, eyes full of concern.

"No, not yet. Jackson is out looking for him." Natalie sighed as she sat down at the kitchen table. "I don't know how he could let this happen, Lace."

"Dave?" Lacey clarified.

Natalie inclined her head before looking down into her glass of water. She spoke in a hushed voice so Emma, who was glued to her cartoon, wouldn't hear. "He had a teenager babysitting while he was at work, *on a Sunday*. There are no toys here, no children's books. There isn't a single healthy thing to eat. What is he even thinking?"

"I know he's the kids' dad, and you loved him once, but

Natalie, he's a textbook narcissist. It's one of the first personality disorders we studied. He never cared what you wanted, only that you made him look better. He doesn't know how to be a good parent because all he sees are two tiny humans whose presence somehow makes him a familyman in name only."

Natalie knew Lacey was right. She couldn't believe how blind she'd been all these years, thinking Dave could ever be the husband and father they needed.

"Think about it—was he ever a parent to them? Did he ever cook for them? Clean up after them? Play with them?"

"No. I did it all," Natalie admitted. Dave had never changed a diaper, never dried a tear. She'd just been brainwashed into thinking it was her job as their mother.

"What am I supposed to do? I can't let them come here twice a month to be cared for by random strangers, but if I ask for full custody, I know he'll fight me on it. It'd be too big of a hit to his ego to let them go."

"Maybe not if you make it about him. Show him he'll look better to his bosses without them taking up his time."

Natalie's phone beeped with a text message. "It's Jackson. He found Noah at the park." Natalie let out a sigh of relief.

"How are things with your super hunky boss-boyfriend?" Lacey asked inquisitively.

"He asked me to move in with him," Natalie responded shyly. She knew her best friend wouldn't judge her, but without being able to explain their newly formed mate bond, she also knew it would still sound completely insane.

"Already? He's not wasting any time, is he?"

"I said yes," Natalie answered. "I can't explain it, Lace. I know it's fast. It just feels so right."

"Have you...?" Lacy waggled her eyebrows. Natalie

blushed. "I *knew* it! He couldn't keep his eyes—or hands—off you. How was it?"

"It was...unbelievable. I've never experienced anything like it," Natalie said as the door opened again.

Jackson walked in with Noah. He gave her a knowing smirk, having heard what she said, and she blushed again. Her embarrassment was short-lived as she rushed to hug Noah.

"Noah, baby, what happened? I was so worried."

Noah looked up to Jackson, who gave him an encouraging nod. "Remember what we talked about, champ."

Natalie gave Jackson an inquisitive look but he just shrugged and indicated Noah should continue.

"I don't want to come back here, Mom. Dad just worked all weekend and there's nothing to do here. The babysitter's mean and I'm hungry. Can we just go home?"

"We'll go home, buddy, but I made an agreement with your dad that you'd come every other weekend. I'll talk to him so it'll be better next time."

"No, Mom, I don't want to come back," Noah cried. "I just want to stay with you and Jackson."

Natalie hugged Noah tighter. Her heart broke as Noah sobbed in her arms. She knew this situation wasn't right, but she wasn't sure what she could do about it. She wasn't confident she could win a court case, and the last thing she wanted to do was take her kids away from their dad, but if he wasn't willing to change, she may not have a choice.

Before Natalie could pull her thoughts together, Dave came storming through the door.

"This is ridiculous. I'm not staying out of my own apartment!" he shouted. His eyes darted from Lacey, who was now sitting on the couch with Emma and holding back a snicker, to Jackson, who stood stone-faced with his arms crossed, and finally to Natalie, who was still holding a sniffling Noah. "Oh good, it's a party. Was anyone going to tell me they found my son?"

"Who should I have called? Your assistant, or the teenage babysitter you left to watch our children all weekend?" Natalie snapped.

Natalie didn't miss the pleading look Noah gave Jackson, but before she could apologize, Jackson spoke up. "Natty, why don't I take the kids to get something to eat while you two talk?"

"That's a great idea. Thank you," Natalie responded, relieved she wouldn't have to do this in front of the kids. "Emma, honey, grab your jacket and go with Jackson."

"Can we get party pancakes?" Emma asked hopefully.

That girl and her pancakes.

Jackson chuckled and replied, "We'll see what we can find." He whispered to Natalie as he moved past her toward the door, "You'll be okay?"

"Yes," she answered softly, not wanting her voice to waver as she prepared to confront Dave.

"Just call if you need me," Jackson added before kissing her cheek and reaching for the door.

"I'll walk out with you," Lacey called out. She leaned in to Natalie and whispered, "I'm really happy for you. Don't let Dave be a bully. You've got this," before following Jackson and the kids out.

Then it was just Dave and Natalie.

Natalie took a deep breath, thinking about what she wanted to say. Before she could get herself together, Dave spoke, and his words reminded her of everything she needed to say.

"Well, if you've got everything handled, I need to get back to work."

Natalie's jaw dropped. "No, Dave. I do not have it *handled*. Do you even care that your son went missing today and you weren't here? You have them every other weekend and you can't rearrange your schedule to spend a little bit of time with your kids?"

"Come on, Lee, you know I'm trying to make partner," Dave whined, as if that excused everything.

"Please, don't call me Lee," Natalie scolded. She had spent ten years stuffing herself in a box, doing everything to make life easier for her husband and children. She didn't have to do that anymore. She knew she would never have to hide herself with Jackson. Knowing that gave her the courage to let herself out of her box with Dave as well.

Dave looked momentarily taken aback. He wasn't used to this Natalie. She took his surprise as an opportunity to continue.

"If becoming a partner is so important to you, maybe it would be easier if you didn't have to worry about the kids."

"What are you saying Le—Natalie? You want to take my kids from me? *He's* putting you up to this, isn't he?" Dave wouldn't even say Jackson's name.

"No, Dave, I don't *want* to take your kids from you. And Jackson has nothing to do with this. I just want my children —*our* children—safe and cared for. If they're just going to be here with a babysitter, wouldn't it be easier if they just stayed with me? You could visit whenever you have the time. Or I can bring them to see you."

Natalie watched as her words sunk in. Dave's eyes closed as he rubbed his hand over his face and sighed deeply. When he made eye contact again, she knew she had him. She smiled and added sweetly, "Maybe it can be different later on, but if taking the kids off your plate will help you make partner, I'm happy to make it work."

Dave shook his head but stated, "Fine. Can you get their things and lock up? I need to be at the office. I'll call you when I can set up a visit." He started out the door.

Natalie called out, "Don't you want to say goodbye to the kids?" But Dave was already gone.

She packed up the kids bags, left a note with their new address, and went to find her family.

Jackson

Jackson had found a restaurant down the street that served their own version of party pancakes, even if it was late afternoon. He'd just ordered for the kids and himself when he received a text from Natalie.

> I hope you enjoyed your weekend alone with me because we won't be getting another one anytime soon.

> What happened? Where are you? Are you okay?

> I'm fine. I'm at the truck. I wanted to tell you first before we tell the kids, but Dave agreed to giving me full custody with him having visitation rights, which at this point, I doubt he'll bother with. I hope that's okay with you.

> Natty, you know that's perfectly okay with me. I can't wait to spend more time with the kids.

> Also, I have a whole family of babysitters, so don't worry. I'll still get to have you to myself on occasion.

> Where are you guys? I'll meet you.

Jackson sent Natalie his location and let the waitress know they had another joining them. He watched the kids color on their menus while they waited.

Jackson knew this wasn't easy for Natalie. He knew she didn't want to take the kids from their father, but she would be anxious wondering if they were with a stranger every time they went. The kids weren't comfortable there, either. This would be a better situation for all of them.

Natalie's relief washed over Jackson when she walked into the restaurant and saw them. Since their mating, he could feel all of her emotions as strongly as if they were his own. The closer she was, the stronger they were. She kissed each kid on the head before sliding in the booth next to Jackson.

"Doing okay?" he asked as he kissed her head.

Natalie sighed. "All this change is overwhelming, but in a good way." Her voice lowered to a whisper. "I need to tell them everything. They've been through so much already."

Jackson gave her thigh a reassuring squeeze. "Let's do it together."

"Hey, kiddos," Natalie started. "While you were at Daddy's, I got to visit Jackson's house, and he asked if maybe we all wanted to move into it with him."

"Move again?" Noah asked warily.

"You guys would each have your own room that you can decorate however you want. There's a big backyard to play in, and it has a barn so we can even get some animals. This would be our last move for a long, long time. We can go see it when we're done here. What do you think?"

"Will we have a new school?" Emma asked.

"No," Natalie answered. "It's not very far from our house now, so you would still go to the same school."

"Can my room be pink?"

Jackson smiled. He'd known Emma wouldn't be hard to convince. It was Noah that would be the harder sell. "Your room is already pink," Jackson replied.

"Yes!" Emma cheered.

"What about you, champ? Think we can try it out?" Jackson questioned, his eyebrows raised.

"Yeah, I guess." Noah shrugged.

When Natalie's hand sought his for support, Jackson squeezed gently as their fingers intertwined, letting her know he was with her in every way.

"There's one more thing I need to tell you." Natalie's voice quivered. "You won't be going to stay at your dad's anymore. Dad will try to visit, or I will bring you to visit him if he has time. But you'll be staying with Jackson and me full-time."

Jackson could see the tension leave Noah. Staying with his dad had made the boy really uncomfortable. Noah looked up at his mother just as the waitress delivered their food. "Thank you," he said before diving into his pancakes.

Jackson smiled at Natalie. She responded with the sweetest smile and he knew everything would be okay. They were going to be together as a family, and to him, nothing could be better than that.

Chapter Twenty-Seven

Natalie

Natalie and Jackson spent the next week packing and moving boxes out to their new home. Any remaining concerns the kids had about moving disappeared when they saw the house. They were already making plans for tree houses and puppies. By the weekend, Natalie's rental was empty and their new home was full of boxes.

The following Sunday morning had them loaded into Jackson's truck for his surprise trip. Emma was rambling in the new pink booster seat that Jackson had bought for his truck, and Noah had his nose buried in yet another comic. They were having trouble finding stories he hadn't read.

Natalie had no idea where Jackson was taking them, but he promised the kids would enjoy it. As they turned down a familiar dirt road, Emma started shouting, "Mommy! It's the orchard! Are we going to see the goats?"

Jackson looked at Natalie, surprised. "You've been here?"

"Yes," Natalie answered. "Lacey and I brought the kids a couple of weeks ago—the weekend before my interview."

Jackson looked perplexed but didn't say a word as he drove past the public parking lot and up to the house at the rear of the property. Natalie remembered a campfire conversation that seemed so far back in her memory—Jackson's parents owned an orchard. This orchard.

Jackson

Something pulled at Jackson like a forgotten memory when Natalie said she'd been to his family's orchard. As he drove down the lane toward the house, he thought about the last time he was here and how he'd smelled Natalie amid the apples. He'd thought he was going crazy at the time, but now he knew why. She *had* been here, and he'd just missed her.

When he pulled up to the house, Natalie turned toward him. "This is your parents' house, isn't it?"

Jackson smiled. "Yes. Are you ready? They have dinner every Sunday for the whole family. I called them last weekend and told them I couldn't make it, but that I'd make it up with extra guests today."

"The whole family?" Natalie asked nervously. She let out a sigh. "I guess I'm as ready as I'll ever be," she said before Jackson could answer.

He helped her out of the truck first and then went to

help Emma. Jackson's dad met them on the front porch and a spark of familiarity showed on Natalie's face.

"I'm glad you found what you were looking for," his dad said to Natalie as he gave her a hug.

"I just needed to wait for the right time," Natalie responded.

Jackson raised an eyebrow at the interaction, wondering what his dad's words meant. Natalie seemed to understand. He introduced the kids and Edwin guided them into the house where they met the rest of the family.

The dinner table was loud and full of laughter. As expected, Jackson's sisters were already trying to talk Natalie into a shopping trip. Even the kids were getting along. When Jackson's mom left the table for the kitchen to get dessert, Jackson followed to help.

"Natalie seems lovely, and her kids are adorable. They're the perfect little family for you," Marie told him as she cut the apple crisp.

"Thanks, Mom. I'm pretty fond of them myself. I never thought I'd have this...what you and dad have. It didn't seem like it was in the cards for me."

"Aww, honey, I always knew you'd find someone special." Marie stopped cutting the crisp and pulled a box out from a drawer in the kitchen. "I want you to have this. Give it to Natalie when she's ready—though, by the way she looks at you, I think she already is."

Jackson opened the box to find his mother's engagement ring. It was a radiant-cut diamond with smaller diamonds fanned out, like leaves set into a gold band.

"Are you sure you want me to have this? What about the girls? Won't they want it?" He wasn't expecting this today.

"Sarah is already married, and I have your grandmother's ring for Isa if she wants it. This ring was meant for Natalie."

"You really think she's ready? I know we're already mates, and she's decided to move in, but isn't it too soon?"

"If it's anything like when your father claimed me, she was ready the moment your teeth hit her neck."

"Eww, Mom. I did *not* need that image," Jackson teased. "Thank you," he said more sincerely.

Jackson stuck the box in his pocket and hugged his mom. They carried dessert out together.

Over at the kids' table, Amber and Rosalie were arguing about who got the bigger piece of apple crisp. All of a sudden, Amber disappeared and a little white wolf pup stood in her place, yipping and snapping at Rosalie. Emma let out a startled screech. Jackson reacted quickly, grabbing the wolf pup by the scruff of her neck. He stood, holding the squirming pup, while everyone else just stared.

After a moment, Sarah broke the silence. "Well, that's new."

Everyone broke out in laughter except for Leah, who ran from the room. Travis followed after her. Jackson had assumed his brother had shared the family secret when they got engaged, but it seemed he was wrong.

Jackson deposited the pup into her mother's arms, where she shifted back to a little girl. Sarah took her off to find some clothes, as hers were torn on the floor.

He then looked to Emma and Noah to see their reaction. Noah's eyes were wide with wonder, but Emma hid hers in her hands in fear.

Noah looked at his sister and then at Jackson, asking without words to share what he knew with his sister. Jackson nodded to Noah, who leaned over to Emma and explained what Jackson, and now Amber, was.

"It's okay, Emma. She's just a wolf shifter. Jackson is, too. Just like in *The Wolf Prince*."

Jackson smiled as he and Natalie worked their way over to Emma. The kids had been asking for Jackson to tell them the story of *The Wolf Prince* every night since he and Natalie got together.

"That's right, little duck. Just like *The Wolf Prince*. My dad is a shifter too."

Edwin joined them, placing a hand on Jackson's shoulder. Jackson could see the pride in his father's eyes as he shared the story he was told as a child.

"Jackson's like *The Wolf Prince*?" Emma asked her mother, dropping her hands from her face. Natalie smiled and gave her a nod. Emma's eyes popped as realization set in. "Does that mean Mommy is your perfect princess?" she asked Jackson.

"She's the most perfect princess," Jackson answered as he wrapped his arm around Natalie and kissed her head.

The dinner party moved outside to the orchard. The apple season was nearing an end, but they had opened the pumpkin patch and the corn maze. Isaac and Isabella took the kids to feed the goats and ponies while the rest of the family sat on the porch, talking and getting to know Natalie.

When the orchard closed to the public, everyone stood around in front of the house while Edwin taught Amber how to shift. In their wolf forms, they played and pounced. Edwin's wolf was a darker gray than Jackson's, but with the same white accents.

Jackson wrapped his arms around Natalie as they watched the two wolves play. She spoke without looking at him. "I want this. The big family. Sunday dinners. I want it all."

Jackson knew then that his mother was right—Natalie

was ready. He knew that the mating bond was stronger than any legally binding ceremony, but suddenly he couldn't wait to marry her, anyway.

"Take a walk with me? The kids are in good hands." Emma was on Isaac's shoulders and Noah sat along the fence, admiring the wolves. Natalie nodded and Jackson pulled her by the hand into the rows of apple trees.

The leaves had mostly turned, but Jackson stopped in front of a tree with a single red apple. Natalie gazed at the apple, grinning.

"What are you thinking about? Or do you always smile at apples?" Jackson teased.

"When we brought the kids here, there was a tree with a single green apple. Something about it called to me. A man came up and told me it wasn't ready."

"Dad." Jackson knew there was a story behind their earlier interaction.

"Yes, though I didn't know that then. He told me that sometimes we find something that feels right but we aren't ready for it, and that if it's meant for us, we'll find it again at the right time." She smiled again, still looking at the apple. "I'm just so glad I found *you* again at the right time."

The right time. It was like a sign from Fate. Jackson could feel the love radiating from her. He picked the apple, handed it to Natalie, then dropped to one knee. Natalie turned to look at him as he pulled out the box his mother had given him.

"I love you, Natty. You and your little family—our little family—have made me the happiest wolf. I know it's soon, but for me, the time couldn't feel more right. You're already my mate, but I want to make you my wife. Will you marry me?"

Natalie's pulse jumped. Jackson got nervous, scared that

he had misjudged the timing. The doubts of it being too soon crept back into his mind. It was only for a moment, until Natalie gave her answer.

"Yes. Of course, I will, Jackson," she said without hesitation. He had just moved to put the ring on her finger when she added, "Under one condition." He looked at her with slight worry in his eyes. She smiled. "We get married here, at the orchard, in the spring."

Jackson put the ring on her before sweeping her up in a kiss. It was a perfect fit. Once again, his mother was right—the ring was made for Natalie.

His eyes were aglow as he set her down with a mischievous grin before stripping off his clothes and shifting to his wolf. He let out a gleeful howl at the moon. A big, deep howl and a tiny, stuttering howl joined him.

I love you so much, my mate, Jackson thought. Natalie's eyes widened and the biggest smile lit up her face.

"I love you too, my wolf," Natalie responded. She'd heard his thoughts.

Catch me, he thought again as he took off toward his family, Natalie laughing and chasing behind him through the trees with his clothes in her arms.

Epilogue

Jackson - 2 months later

The snow was starting to move in. Jackson's schedule was light, since most people didn't schedule their routine appointments in the colder months. He thought Natalie was in the supply room doing the year-end inventory, but when he went to find her, the room was empty.

He made his way toward the kennels, where he found her sitting on the floor, surrounded by kittens. Mama Cat, as they'd named her, had her three kittens and they were now ready for their new home—which was, apparently, his barn. Natalie made the argument that every barn needs cats, but something told him they would probably end up in his house.

He stood in the doorway smiling at his mate—his fiance—playing with the little things. At first, they'd growled and hissed at him, but they were slowly warming up.

Jackson was ready to sit down and join the playtime when he heard shouting in the lobby. He made his way to the front to see Cheryl wheeling out their single gurney to the back of a truck. Two men unloaded a large animal onto the gurney and helped bring it through the doors. In the light, Jackson could see that it was a wolf. Not just a wolf, but the shifter from the campground.

Jackson hollered, "Natalie, I need you!"

Then he turned to the men. "What happened here?"

"The roads are getting icy, Doc, and this wolf sprinted out into the road out of nowhere. I hit the brakes but the truck fishtailed right into him. We brought him straight here. He's still breathing but hasn't moved. What's a wolf doing here, anyway?"

"Thank you, gentlemen. We'll get him fixed up." Jackson wheeled the gurney into the exam room and Natalie followed.

"Is that...?" Natalie started.

"It's the shifter that found Noah," Jackson responded. "I have no idea what he's doing here. He'll heal quickly, but that cut on his leg is pretty bad, and we don't want the debris in it to cause an infection. I don't know how he'll react when he wakes up so I'm going to sedate him. Can you get me some hot water and a clean cloth from the cabinet?"

With Natalie's help, Jackson injected the sedative into the shifter. He inspected the rest of his injuries while Natalie cleaned the wound. Jackson used tweezers to pull out some gravel from the cut before stitching it with dissolving stitches. He had to move fast, as the shifter would metabolize the sedative quickly. He injected some antibiotics near the wound and stood back just as the wolf turned into a man.

The shifter opened his eyes and turned his head toward Natalie. Then he opened his mouth and uttered a single word:

"Mate."

Acknowledgments

I want to give a big thank you to all who made writing and publishing this book possible.

First and foremost, thank you to my husband, who has been my sounding board despite knowing nothing about romance novels. He has been wonderfully supportive, giving me the time and resources needed to make my dream of publishing a book a reality.

Thank you to the friends that have listened to me talk about writing and books day in and day out.

Thank you to Bethany, Cruise, Rosemary, and Hannah for being my alpha/beta readers. Your feedback both helped shape the story into something better, as well as gave me confidence to continue writing it.

Thanks to Carly for my beautiful cover designs and working through all my "what if we did this" and "just one more thing" scenarios.

Huge thank you to my editors, Meg and Kay. Your feedback and edits elevated my story in a way I didn't know possible.

Lastly, thank you to my readers for giving this debut author a chance. I hope that you enjoyed Jackson and Natalie's story, and will continue reading the Second Chance Fates series, with Lacey and Derek's story coming soon in Love Again on Wolf Mountain.

What's Next?

For updates, sneak peeks, and bonus content, including a full telling of Jackson's favorite bedtime story "The Wolf Prince," subscribe to my newsletter at the link below or visit https://www.ginnydanesauthor.com.

Ginny Danes Newsletter

About the Author

Ginny Danes has loved writing for her entire life, almost as much as she loves to read. She enjoys writing cozy romance stories that also make you wonder if the paranormal really could exist. Her stories are full of emotion, family, and of course...love.

Ginny lives in Michigan with her husband, twins, and two cats. In her free time she loves reading, crafting, playing video games, going camping, and spending time with family. Her favorite things to read are shifter romance, hockey romance, and anything with dragons.

www.ingramcontent.com/pod-product-compliance
Ingram Content Group UK Ltd.
Pitfield, Milton Keynes, MK11 3LW, UK
UKHW042001230426
12048UKWH00009B/481